WELL, REALLY,
MR. TWIDDLE!

by
ENID BLYTON

WELL, REALLY,
MR. TWIDDLE!

by
ENID BLYTON

This edition © GEORGE NEWNES LIMITED 1968
Published by DEAN & SON, LTD.

Made and Printed in Great Britain by Purnell & Sons, Ltd.
Paulton (Somerset) and London

603 03270 2

CONTENTS

Well, Really, Mr. Twiddle!

"I'm certainly in luck to-day, wife," said Mr. Twiddle, looking very pleased with himself. "First, I found that nice pencil I lost last week, and then when I went to feed the hens there were five eggs, and now the postman has brought me a present from my sister Hannah—a nice new hat!"

He tried it on. It certainly was a nice hat. Mrs. Twiddle wanted to put a little brown hen-feather in the band, but Mr. Twiddle wouldn't let her.

"No. I don't like feathers in hats," he said. "If only I had a nice new suit now, to go with my hat. I *should* look smart!"

"Well, as you're having such a lucky day you might find one lying in the road," said Mrs. Twiddle, with a giggle.

"You simply never know what might happen when your luck is in," said Twiddle. "I wouldn't be a bit surprised if I found a five-pound note when I was out walking this morning."

"Well, you'd have to take it to the police station and hand it in to the police, and tell them to find the owner," said Mrs. Twiddle.

"Ah, but as my luck is in they wouldn't find the owner, and they would have to give it back to me," said Mr. Twiddle, still admiring himself in his new hat.

"You've got it on back to front, but I suppose you don't really mind that," said Mrs. Twiddle, with another little giggle.

A timid knock came at the door, and a little girl's head peeped in. "Please, Mrs. Twiddle, may I borrow your cat to play with this morning?"

"Certainly, dear," said Mrs. Twiddle. "Call her. She does so love playing with a kind little girl like you."

Mr. Twiddle watched the little girl carry the purring cat away, and he looked very pleased. "Well, if that isn't *another* bit of luck!" he said. "We've got rid of that cat for a whole morning. Now I can walk about the house without falling over it."

"I don't know why you don't like our dear old

cat," said Mrs. Twiddle. "You're the only person who ever falls over it, anyway."

"And do you know why?" said Mr. Twiddle, suddenly looking rather fierce. "I'll tell you! It's because I'm the only person that cat tries to trip up! She's always walking through my legs! Bit of good luck, I tell you, Puss going off with Polly."

"Well, if you don't go and get the fish for dinner your good luck will come to an end, because you'll go hungry," said Mrs. Twiddle, looking at the clock. "Put on your old hat, Twiddle, and get the shopping basket, do. Take some paper with you for the fish."

Twiddle fetched the basket. He put a newspaper in it to wrap the fish in when he bought it. But he didn't change his nice new hat for his old one. No, he thought he looked so nice in the new one that he felt he might as well give everyone a treat when they looked at him!

"Put your *old* hat on!" called Mrs. Twiddle, when she saw him going out with his new one on his head.

"No, no, dear," said Mr. Twiddle, trying to find a quick reason for keeping it on. "I told you my luck is in to-day—suppose I find a nice new suit somewhere. I'd look dreadful if I didn't have a nice hat to wear with it."

"Don't be silly, Twiddle!" called his wife, but by that time he was out of the front gate and couldn't hear her. He hurried along to the fishshop.

He stood in the queue for ten minutes and then got a large piece of rather smelly cod. He had it wrapped carefully in the newspaper, and hoped that he wouldn't be followed home by half a dozen cats.

"I won't go home through the village in case the cats smell the fish and come after me," thought Twiddle, remembering how annoyed he had been last time by having five cats trailing after him all the way home, sniffing the kippers in his basket. "I'll go back through the wood."

So he took the other way home and wandered along in the wood, enjoying the smell of the hawthorn blossom and the sight of the bluebells. It was a very hot day, and Mr. Twiddle was glad he hadn't got an overcoat on.

Then he saw a most extraordinary sight. He stopped and looked as if he couldn't believe his eyes. Neatly folded up under a bush was a suit of beautiful new clothes!

Twiddle stood and stared and his heart began to thump in excitement. There! What had he said that very morning! His luck was certainly in, because here was a new suit of clothes waiting to go with his nice new hat!

"But, wait, Twiddle," said Twiddle to himself, cautiously. "They might belong to someone, you know. Have a look around and see."

So he had a good look round, but he could see nobody at all. He went back to the neat pile of clothes and looked at them. Coat, trousers, waist-coat, vest, socks, braces . . . why, there was every-thing except a hat!

"This is most extraordinary," said Twiddle. "It just shows what can happen when your luck is in! I get a new hat from Hannah—and, lo and behold, I find a complete set of new clothes to go with it, and nobody to own them!"

He looked at them again. They were exactly his size. They were *meant* for him! He looked at the collar of the suit, half expecting to see his own name marked there, and was quite disappointed when it wasn't. But, would you believe it, on the neat white handkerchief folded inside the left-hand top pocket of the coat was the letter T in pale blue thread! Twiddle stared in the greatest delight.

"That proves it," he said. "Absolutely. Completely. No doubt whatever. This certainly is my lucky morning! Goodness knows what I shall find next!"

He picked up the clothes and was about to put them into his basket when he remembered the fish. "Better undo the fish, take a bit of the paper and wrap up the clothes in it or they'll smell of fish," said Twiddle, forgetting that the paper must smell very strongly of fish already.

He wrapped the clothes up carefully in some of the newspaper, and then made his way home, wondering what bit of good luck would happen to him next. "I shall put on this new suit as soon as I get home," thought Mr. Twiddle, "and wear it with my new hat. How grand I shall look!"

He was longing to tell his wife of his new piece of luck, and he was disappointed when he got home and found that she was out. He went to get himself some lemonade to drink, and then heard Mrs. Twiddle at the front door. She was talking to somebody.

"Bother! She's brought a visitor home," thought Mr. Twiddle, who didn't like his wife's visitors very much because they talked such a lot.

Then he got a terrible shock. Mrs. Twiddle brought her visitor into the kitchen, and Twiddle could hardly believe his eyes when he saw a poor, shivering, dripping man in a wet bathing-suit! He gaped at him in surprise.

"Twiddle! I met this poor fellow running down the street in an awful state," said Mrs. Twiddle. "He thought he would bathe in the Blue Pool because it was so hot to-day, so he took his bathing-suit and went to the wood. He took off his nice new clothes, hid them under a bush, and went to bathe."

"And w-w-when I c-c-c-came b-b-b-back, they had been t-t-taken by a r-r-robber!" said the shivering man, standing as close to the kitchen fire as he could.

"So, Twiddle, I brought the poor fellow in here, and I thought you could lend him a suit," said Mrs. Twiddle, "and I thought I'd give him a good hot meal, or he'll get a terrible cold, and then perhaps you'd go along to the police station with him and tell the police about the robbery. I mean, a man who is hateful enough to take a bather's clothes deserves to go to prison at once!"

Twiddle's heart went right down into his boots and stayed there. He stared at his wife in such a peculiar way that she thought he must be ill. He couldn't say a single word.

But he thought a lot! "Oh, dear! So they were

his clothes—and he was bathing! Why didn't I think of the Blue Pool? Oh, dear, oh, dear—I hope Mrs. Twiddle doesn't look in the basket yet and find the clothes. What am I to *do*?"

"Twiddle, don't stand there gaping like a moonstruck goldfish!" said Mrs. Twiddle, sharply. "Go and get an old suit of clothes, quickly. Do you want this poor fellow to die of cold?"

Mr. Twiddle wasn't sure if he did or not, he felt in such a terrible muddle. He went upstairs to think it over, but then came down again very quickly when he remembered he had left the basket in the scullery with the fish and the suit there. He must certainly hide that basket!

He snatched up the basket, opened the scullery window and dropped the basket and its contents neatly outside under a lilac bush. There! They would be safe there till he could think what was best to do.

"Twiddle! What in the world are you doing in the scullery?" called his wife. "You don't keep your clothes *there*! They're in the cupboard upstairs."

Twiddle shot upstairs. He sank down on his bed. What could he do? What could he say? Nobody would believe him if he said he had thought that finding those clothes was just a bit of the good luck he had had that day. He could see himself now that it had been a very silly thing to think. But he really had thought it.

"If I go down and give him his right clothes, he might quite well haul me off to the police station and put me into prison," thought poor Mr. Twiddle. "And if I don't give him them I shall feel really awful. He's got to have them back somehow."

Mrs. Twiddle shouted upstairs: "TWIDDLE! *Will* you bring some clothes down at once for this poor shivering fellow? I'm just going to cook dinner quickly, so that he can have something hot. Where's the fish?"

Now Twiddle was in another muddle. The fish was in the basket underneath the lilac bush outside the scullery window. But he couldn't say that, of course. He seemed to be getting deeper and deeper into trouble. He scrabbled hastily in the cupboard and took down an armful of clothes. Mrs. Twiddle gave them to the wet, shivering bather, and shut him into the drawing-room to change.

"Where's the fish?" she said to Twiddle, sharply.

"Er—now let me see," said Twiddle looking very vague. "Now—just let me see."

A miaow suddenly came from the scullery next to the kitchen. "There's Puss back again," said Mrs. Twiddle, and she looked pleased. "Open the kitchen door and let her in, Twiddle. She's a real home-cat—never stays away for long!"

Twiddle opened the door, feeling that his good luck had completely vanished. The cat appeared, dragging behind it a pair of fishy-smelling trousers!

Twiddle stared at the cat with great dislike. He knew at once what had happened. That tiresome animal had come home, smelt the fish in the basket lying under the clothes, and had scrabbled about in the paper and brought in the trousers, because they now smelt so deliciously of fish.

"Well! Look at that!" said Mrs. Twiddle, in the greatest astonishment. "Whatever will the cat bring in next? A pair of trousers! Where did she get them from?"

The cat disappeared, and came back again dragging a coat, which also smelt very strongly of fish. Mrs. Twiddle began to think she must be in some kind of peculiar dream made up of shivering bathers, fishy clothes and a cat that came in and out with them.

Then the drawing-room door flew open and out came the bather, looking very different in Twiddle's old suit, which fitted him perfectly. He stood still and stared when he saw his coat and trousers over Mrs. Twiddle's arm—and then stared even more when the cat reappeared, dragging a pair of fishy socks.

"I say—look—they're my clothes the cat is bringing in," stammered the man, in amazement.

"*Your* clothes? Your c-c-c . . ." stammered Mrs. Twiddle, thinking that her dream was turning into a nightmare. "But how could Puss find them? Oh, goodness me, now she's bringing in a vest!"

The man picked up all his clothes. Mr. Twiddle

forced himself to speak in an ordinary kind of voice, though he was trembling inside. "Well—if they're your clothes, perhaps you'd like to go back into the drawing-room again, take off my suit, and put your own on."

"No," said the man, decidedly, sniffing at his clothes. "They smell of fish. I couldn't possibly wear them till the smell is gone. If you don't mind, I'll wear yours till to-morrow, then put my own on. I'll return yours then. I'll go now—but I wish I knew where your cat got my clothes from."

He went out of the front door and banged it shut. Mrs. Twiddle stared at Mr. Twiddle, feeling rather faint. She sat down in her rocking-chair. "Oh, Twiddle! I don't understand this at all. I feel quite queer. How did Puss get those clothes? Do you think she was clever enough to understand all we said, and went to hunt for them and found them?"

"No, I don't," said Twiddle. "It was just a bit of that cat's usual interference. She . . ."

Mrs. Twiddle alarmed him by suddenly leaping

to her feet with a yell. "Look! The cat's got the fish! Is that the fish you brought home for dinner, Twiddle? Oh, she's stolen it—she's over the wall by now. Twiddle, where did you put that fish, you silly, stupid fellow?"

"It was in the basket—er—under the lilac bush," said poor Twiddle.

Mrs. Twiddle looked at him as if he was quite mad. "Under the *lilac* bush! But WHY? Have you gone mad, Twiddle? You'd better go to bed, I think. You must be ill."

Twiddle thought that bed would be a very nice peaceful place, and he went up very thankfully. There was no dinner because the cat had taken the fish, but Mr. Twiddle didn't mind that. It was nice to be able to pretend to be asleep, and not be asked any more awkward questions. *What* a good thing the cat had found the clothes and brought them in, after all! Now nobody would ever know the silly thing he had done in taking them home himself.

But Twiddle is going to get a shock—because that bather isn't going to come back with Twiddle's old suit! He's a dishonest fellow, and he's going to keep it. But how can Twiddle go to the police and complain about *that*? Didn't he do exactly the same thing himself, when he thought his luck was in?

Poor old Twiddle! He's not so lucky, after all!

2

Mr. Twiddle's Christmas Mistake

MR. TWIDDLE was feeling very happy. It was almost Christmas time. He had made some really beautiful Christmas cards, and had painted them himself. Most of them had robins and holly on them, because those were the two things he drew the best.

He had a cupboard full of parcels. He was going to give Mrs. Twiddle a lot of nice surprises on Christmas Day. And he had bought twelve circus tickets.

Three days before Christmas the circus was coming to Twiddle's town. Twiddle loved a circus, especially one with elephants in it, and this one had three.

So he had saved up his money and had bought twelve tickets, two for himself and his wife, and ten for all their grandchildren. What a treat for them, to be sure!

"Shan't I feel grand going to the circus with ten boys and girls!" said Mr. Twiddle to his wife

for about the twentieth time. "Shan't we laugh at
the clowns! And clap the elephants."

"You'll enjoy it all more than the children will,
I should think," said Mrs. Twiddle; and she
laughed. Sometimes she thought dear old Twiddle
had never grown up.

"I'd better write the names and addresses on my
Christmas cards this evening and post them," said
Mr. Twiddle, four days before Christmas. "We
are asked to post early. Yes, I had better do that.
Will you lend me your pen, wife?"

"Oh, dear, have you lost yours again?" said
Mrs. Twiddle. "I wonder where it is this time?
Yes, I'll lend you mine, Twiddle, but please don't
do with it what you did last time."

"Why, what did I do?" asked Twiddle surprised.

"You left it sticking into the vase of flowers,"
said Mrs. Twiddle, "and I didn't find it till
I emptied them when they were dead. I suppose
you thought you had stuck it into the ink-
pot."

"I'll be careful this time," said Twiddle. He sat
down at the table. He spread out all the circus

tickets to look at them once more. How lovely! Twelve of them!

Then he began on his cards. He wrote the names and addresses very neatly indeed. He had done the pictures on post cards, so all he had to do was to write the address on each and stamp it.

"Now don't you be too long over those cards," said Mrs. Twiddle, looking at the clock. "I shall want the table for supper in half an hour."

"I'll be finished long before that," said Twiddle, dipping his pen into his wife's little box of pins, thinking it was the ink. "Dear me—how silly of me!"

Twiddle was longer than he had expected. He had to let the cat in when she came scratching at the door. Then he had to let the dog out. Then no sooner had he sat down again than the dog wanted to come in and the cat decided to go out.

"Those animals want a footman to wait on them," grumbled Mr. Twiddle. "Lie down, dog!"

"He wants a drink of water," said Mrs. Twiddle. "His bowl's empty. He's thirsty, Twiddle."

"So am I," said Twiddle, shaking a blot off his pen. "My glass is empty. But I've got no one who will jump up and fill it for me unless I do it myself. So the dog can wait, too. He never does a thing for me. I'm always waiting on him."

Well, what with one thing and another, Twiddle hadn't finished by the time Mrs. Twiddle wanted the table. So he had to hurry up at the last, and he stacked all the circus tickets together and piled his Christmas cards in another heap.

"I'll go out and post the cards while you're laying the supper, wife," he said.

"Well, take the dog for a walk," said Mrs. Twiddle. "He'll be pleased."

"I just wait on that dog hand and foot," grumbled Mr. Twiddle. "And all he does is to lie about where I can keep falling over him."

"You'd better hurry up, or you'll miss the post," said Mrs. Twiddle. "You've only got a few minutes."

Twiddle snatched up the pile of cards and went out. The dog went too. The cat came in as they went out and lay down by the fire. Twiddle almost fell over her.

"Why can't you look where you're going?" said Mrs. Twiddle.

"Well, why doesn't the cat look where *she's* going?" asked Twiddle crossly, pulling on his coat. "Come on, dog."

He went into the darkness. He was soon back. The cat thought it would go out as he came in, and he nearly fell over it again. He glared at the cat's tail. "I believe she does it on purpose," he said.

"No," said Mrs. Twiddle. "It's just that you are stupid, Twiddle, dear."

"Stupid!" cried Twiddle, losing his temper. "I like *that*! I'm the cleverest person in this house, let me tell you. Where would you all be without me? And who thought of taking all our grand-children to the circus to-morrow, I'd like to know? Why, all you could think of for a Christmas treat for them was— ---"

"All right, all right, Twiddle," said Mrs. Twiddle, putting a pie down on the table with a bang. "I agree that you're the cleverest man in the town. By the way, what did you do with my pen?"

It wasn't to be found. Oh, dear, Twiddle didn't feel quite so clever, after all. He sat down to his supper gloomily. Mrs. Twiddle wondered what to say to put him into a good temper again. She looked round, and saw a pile of Christmas cards on the dresser. That was why he was in such a bad temper, perhaps.

"I'm sorry you missed the post, Twiddle," she said.

Mr. Twiddle stared at her in surprise. "I didn't miss it," he said.

"Oh! Then why didn't you post your Christmas cards?" asked Mrs. Twiddle.

"I did," said Twiddle, thinking that his wife must be a little mad. "I posted all of them, I heard them go into the pillar-box—slip-slap."

"How extraordinary!" said Mrs. Twiddle, looking round at the Christmas cards again. "Then why did you bring them back? How did you get them out of the post-box?"

Mr. Twiddle gasped. Yes—there was no doubt about it. Mrs. Twiddle must either be ill or mad. He got up and patted her on the back.

"There, there!" he said. "Do you feel all right, love? Have you got a bad headache? There, there!"

"Don't 'there, there' me like that," said Mrs. Twiddle, annoyed. "I'm not feeling bad. All I want to know is—why did you go out to post your Christmas cards and come back with them, and yet keep on telling me you heard them go slip-slap down into the box?"

WRT—B

Then poor Twiddle caught sight of the pile of Christmas cards on the dresser. He stared at them. He began to wonder if he had gone mad! Hadn't he just been to post them—and hadn't he heard them go into the box—and yet here they were under his very nose! He sat down, feeling quite peculiar.

There was a little silence. Mrs. Twiddle looked at Twiddle sharply. "Twiddle," she said, "where are the circus tickets?"

"Er—er—I left them in a neat pile on the dresser," said Twiddle, and he looked for them. But they weren't there.

"Well, the cat hasn't eaten them," said Mrs. Twiddle. "What have you done with them?"

Poor Twiddle gave a sudden groan. "Oh, my, oh, my! I've posted them, instead of my Christmas cards! I was in such a hurry—and what with the dog going out and the cat coming in, and——"

"Don't make excuses," said Mrs. Twiddle. "For a man who thinks himself the cleverest in this town you're not very bright to-night, Twiddle. Now, we shan't be able to go to the circus!"

"Perhaps the postman hasn't collected the letters yet," said Twiddle, getting up and fetching his coat. "I'll go and see. I'll run all the way."

The dog went with him, pleased at an extra run. He got under Twiddle's feet as usual, but Twiddle hadn't any breath to scold him. He got to the post-box—and oh, cheers, there was the postman, just emptying the box!

"I've made a mistake!" panted Twiddle. "I've

posted some tickets. Ah, yes, there they are! Could you give them me back, please?"

The postman laughed. He picked out the circus tickets and gave them to Twiddle. "Good thing you just caught me," he said. "It would have been a pity to miss the circus. Good night, sir."

Twiddle was so pleased. He rushed back home. "I've got the tickets," he said. "We're all right for the circus!"

"It's a pity you forgot to take your cards to post them just now," said Mrs. Twiddle. "Still, never mind, they'll probably get there on New Year's Day. Sit down and have a cup of tea now, and finish your meal. Give me the tickets. The next thing you'll be doing is lighting the kitchen fire with them!"

Twiddle stirred his tea hard. Mrs. Twiddle looked at him.

"So that's where my pen went!" she said. "You're stirring your tea with it, Twiddle. Well, well—I'll give you a spoon to write with next time! What *is* to be done with you?"

I don't know. Do you?

3

Mr. Twiddle Forgets

"Twiddle, it's the New Year to-morrow," said Mrs. Twiddle, busily darning an enormous hole in one of Mr. Twiddle's socks. "New Year's Eve to-night—the time when people make good resolutions."

"What exactly is a resolution?" asked Mr. Twiddle. "It's such a long and peculiar word."

"Well—when you make a resolution it just means that you resolve to do something and really mean it," said Mrs. Twiddle. "Don't pretend you don't know that, Twiddle! You make a promise to yourself—you determine to do something; but if you make this resolution on New Year's Eve it's very important and very special."

"Oh!" said Twiddle. "Have *you* made any good resolutions, wife?"

"Dear me, yes," said Mrs. Twiddle. "I've resolved not to be cross with the paper-boy when he brings the wrong paper—and I've resolved to mend all those old shirts of yours I've been putting off for so long—and I've resolved not to let you snore at nights——"

"Well! What a queer resolution!" said Mr. Twiddle, indignantly. "Surely that ought to be *my* resolution, not yours, wife?"

"Oh, no, dear—because *you* can't stop yourself snoring, and I very well can," said Mrs. Twiddle. "I've only got to pinch you hard and you stop."

"Well, I don't think that's at all a nice resolution to make," said Twiddle.

"Now, now, don't be silly. You think about your own resolutions, not mine," said Mrs. Twiddle.

Twiddle thought. "I've got quite a lot in my mind," he said at last. "I'll remember to chop the wood for you. I'll remember to mend that chair-leg you've been asking me about for ages. I'll resolve to be kinder to the cat—though that will be hard because she honestly does try to trip me up on purpose, I'm sure of it—still, I'll buy her some fish to show her I mean to be kind."

"Miaow," said the cat, thrilled, and dug its claws into Twiddle's ankles as it stretched itself.

"What do you want to do that for, you unkind, horrid creature?" shouted Twiddle, and smacked the cat.

"Well!" said Mrs. Twiddle, in surprise. "I don't think much of your resolutions if you forget them so quickly."

"I haven't forgotten," said Twiddle. "But I haven't begun them yet—it isn't New Year's Day till to-morrow. Now, let me think—I'll make a resolution to wind up the clock—and to paint the shed—and to sweep the kitchen chimney for you—and——"

"Now, Twiddle, it's not a good thing to make so *many* resolutions," said Mrs. Twiddle. "Make ONE—one good sensible one—and keep it."

"All right," said Twiddle, "I will. I know! I'll make a resolution not to forget a single thing! There—now you won't have to keep on telling me what a dreadful memory I have."

"Splendid!" said Mrs. Twiddle. "Now you write down that resolution and put it somewhere to remind you—or else you'll forget it."

So Twiddle wrote out his resolution in his best handwriting. "My New Year's Resolution is that I will not forget a single thing!"

He stood it behind the clock where he could see it. He felt very pleased with himself. Aha! He would show Mrs. Twiddle that he could make just as good resolutions as she could!

Next morning he heard his wife up very early. He called down in astonishment to know why she was up.

"Oh, just one of my good resolutions," said

Mrs. Twiddle. "I've determined I will never be late down in the morning. I hope you've remembered *your* resolution, Twiddle."

Twiddle lay back in bed and thought hard. Now, what *was* his resolution? What could it have been? To be kind to the cat and get her fish? To wind up the clock? To mend something? Now WHAT was that fine, sensible resolution he had made?

He fell asleep trying to remember. It was no use, he just couldn't think of it. He was very late down for breakfast and Mrs. Twiddle was cross.

"Late the first morning of the year! And what about that good resolution of yours? Have you remembered it?"

Well, Mrs. Twiddle was in one of her rather bustling moods, and Twiddle simply didn't dare to tell her he had already forgotten what his good resolution was. "You just wait and see," he told Mrs. Twiddle.

After breakfast he tried again to remember what he had resolved to do. "Was it to chop the wood?" he wondered. "Perhaps it was. I'll do it."

So out he went and chopped a whole lot of wood

for Mrs. Twiddle. She was very pleased. But Twiddle didn't feel that had been his resolution. He tried something else. He stroked the cat and then actually went out to buy it some fish. But no —surely that wasn't his resolution? Mrs. Twiddle didn't say anything to make him think it was.

Twiddle found the broken chair and mended the leg.

Now, surely *that* had been his resolution? Mrs. Twiddle thanked him heartily. But she didn't say it was nice to see he had kept his resolution. So it couldn't be that.

Poor Twiddle! The things he did that day to try and find out what it was he had made a resolution about! He swept both the kitchen and the parlour chimneys and covered himself with soot. He had to have a bath, and he actually remembered to clean it after him—but somehow he didn't feel that had anything to do with his resolution either.

"I believe it was to paint the shed!" thought Mr. Twiddle, and out he went to get a tin of paint and a brush.

Mrs. Twiddle came out to watch. "Well,

you really are good to-day," she said. "And how well you've painted the shed. Anyone would think you had made a good resolution to do it today!"

Oh, dear! So he hadn't made a resolution about painting the shed. Mr. Twiddle felt very gloomy

How many more things was he going to do before he remembered what his resolution really was! If only he could ask Mrs. Twiddle what it was. But she would laugh at him too much. No, he really must remember it himself.

He went in to wash for tea, wondering what else there was for him to do.

Wind up the clock! Yes, of course—perhaps *that* was his good resolution. Twiddle went to the clock on the mantelpiece and hunted for the key. Mrs. Twiddle looked up.

"Reading your good resolution again?" she said.

"What do you mean?" asked Twiddle—and then he suddenly saw the good resolution he had written out so neatly the night before, and stood behind the clock. There it was, staring him in the face—"My New Year's Resolution is that I will not forget a single thing!"

So that was it—dear, dear!—and the first thing he had done was to forget what his resolution had been! Whatever would Mrs. Twiddle say if she knew?

"You've remembered your resolution marvell-ously, I think," she said. "Really marvellously! You haven't forgotten a single thing all day long, Twiddle. I do feel pleased. I shall cook you a very special kipper for your tea!"

He did enjoy his kipper—but, you know, he didn't say a word to Mrs. Twiddle about forgetting his resolution—not one single word. It's still there, behind the clock. I wonder how soon he'll forget it again!

4

Twiddle in Trouble Again

MR. TWIDDLE was sitting by the fire reading his paper. The windows were shut. It was nice and warm and cosy.

Then the cat pushed at the door, opened it wide, and strolled into the room. A cold draught at once blew down Mr. Twiddle's neck.

He looked round, and then spoke crossly to Mrs. Twiddle, who was sitting on the opposite side of the fireplace.

"Wife, I wish you'd teach your cat to shut the door after her. She comes in and leaves it wide open—and *I* have to get up and shut it."

"You can't teach cats things like that," said Mrs. Twiddle, sleepily.

"You can teach dogs all kinds of tricks," grumbled Mr. Twiddle. "Shut the door, Puss!"

The cat sat down and washed itself. It always did that when it saw that Twiddle was cross. It knew it annoyed him.

"Oh, do get up and shut the door, Twiddle," said his wife. "There's such a draught."

Twiddle got up, grumbling. He shut the door and came back to his chair. The cat was now lying on it, fast asleep.

"Look at that!" said Twiddle. "It not only leaves the door open for me to shut, but takes my chair, too, and then pretends to be asleep."

He turned the cat off his chair. It at once went to a window, and mewed. "Let it out, Twiddle, dear," said Mrs. Twiddle.

"But it's only just come in," said Twiddle, exasperated.

"Well, it wants to go out again," said Mrs. Twiddle.

So Twiddle got up, opened the window and let the cat out. He banged the window shut so hard that the cat leapt into the air with fright. So did Mrs. Twiddle.

"Twiddle! Don't do things like that!" she said. "I've told you before, and . . ."

Twiddle sat down and closed his eyes. He thought if he pretended to be asleep, Mrs. Twiddle wouldn't go on scolding him. But she did. However, in a few minutes Twiddle really was asleep.

He was awakened by a very cold draught blowing round his neck. He sat up and looked round. The door was wide open again.

"The cat's just come in," said Mrs. Twiddle. "I expect she found it cold outside to-day, poor lamb. Would you shut the door, Twiddle?"

Then Twiddle lost his temper. He swooped on the astonished cat, caught tight hold of it, and ran upstairs with it. He pushed it into the spare bedroom, where all the windows were tightly closed, and then slammed and locked the door.

"Now, you just stay there, where you can't get out *or* in!" said Twiddle. "Making me open windows and shut doors all the afternoon! Grrrrrrrr!"

The cat settled down in the middle of the eiderdown, purring. Twiddle went downstairs, looking fierce. "Now, wife, listen to me—that cat stays there all the afternoon, do you hear?"

Mrs. Twiddle knew she couldn't do anything

with Twiddle when he really was in a temper, so she didn't say anything at all.

Presently there was a peculiar noise from upstairs. The boards creaked loudly, as if someone was walking over the spare-room floor.

"Whatever's that?" said Mrs. Twiddle, looking alarmed, and she half-rose to go up to see.

"Sit down," said Twiddle. "You know it's the cat. I'm not going to let you go upstairs and let her out. Sit down. She's just walking about."

"But you can't usually hear cats walk!" cried Mrs. Twiddle.

"She's probably stamping around in a temper," said Twiddle. "Sit down!"

Soon there was another noise, as if something was falling. Mrs. Twiddle leapt up. "I must go and see what's happening!"

"SIT DOWN!" roared Twiddle. "It's the cat walking about on the dressing-table, that's all, and knocking over the candlesticks!"

"But the cat never walks on the dressing-table," said Mrs. Twiddle. Still, she sat down, because Twiddle really did look so very fierce.

Presently there was a squeaking noise, and Mrs. Twiddle looked up to the ceiling, above which was the spare room. "What's that?" she said.

"The cat squealing," said Twiddle, pleased. "Let it squeal. Do it good. It's got nobody to open and shut doors and windows for it up there and it's angry."

"But that squeak sounded exactly as if the wardrobe door was being opened," said Mrs. Twiddle, alarmed. "It always squeaks like that."

"Well, I daresay your cat can open wardrobe doors as easily as it can open the kitchen door, and make a draught down my neck," said Twiddle. "Sit down, wife!"

After that there was a curious slithering sound, and then nothing at all. Mrs. Twiddle went on with her knitting. Twiddle fell asleep. But he was awakened once more by a draught blowing down his neck, and when he turned round, there was the door opening wide again—and the cat walking in, purring loudly!

"Puss dear! Clever Puss! How did you get out of the spare room?" said Mrs. Twiddle, pleased. "Twiddle, isn't she clever! How in the world did she manage it?"

Twiddle stared at the cat, astonished and angry. It *couldn't* get out of the spare room—and yet there it was!

"It must be another cat!" said Twiddle at last. "Our own *must* be in the spare room. Why, I *locked* it in!"

Twiddle went up to the spare room. How queer—the door was still locked! And the windows had been closed—so how *could* the cat have got out? He unlocked the door and looked in.

The window was wide open! The wardrobe door was wide open, too—and Twiddle's best coat was gone! The drawers of the chest were open, and Mrs. Twiddle's best bed-cover, which was kept there, was gone. So were the silver candlesticks off the dressing-table, and the clock from the mantelpiece. Oh dear, what could have happened?

Mrs. Twiddle heard Twiddle's groan and came hurrying up. When she saw what had happened, she burst into tears.

"A burglar came! He must have climbed up the gutter-pipe whilst we were in the kitchen, and he tramped about overhead and opened drawers, and knocked things over, and opened the wardrobe door which squeaks—and we heard everything—and you said it was the cat! If you hadn't been unkind to the cat, and shut her in here, and said *she* made all the noise, poor lamb, we'd have shot up to the spare room and caught the burglar at once!"

Twiddle felt very, very uncomfortable. He had to tell the whole story to the police later on, and they tried hard not to laugh.

"I hope you'll never be hard on poor Puss again," said Mrs. Twiddle that evening.

"I wasn't hard on her," said Twiddle. "*She's* hard on *me*—making me shut doors and——"

"Now, that's enough!" said Mrs. Twiddle. "You've done enough damage for *one* day, Twiddle, losing your temper. Don't lose it again. Look, take the cat for me a minute. I've got to peep in the oven."

And will you believe it, poor Twiddle had to nurse the cat the whole evening. She purred so loudly that he couldn't hear the wireless properly. What a shame!

5

Twiddle Cuts the Grass

"I DO wish," said Mrs. Twiddle, "I *do* wish, Twiddle, that you would do something about that long grass in the garden. It looks so very untidy."

Mrs. Twiddle said this almost every day. Mr. Twiddle sighed. He knew he would have to cut that grass sooner or later. Well, it was a nice day. He might as well do it and get it over.

"Very well, my love," he said. "I'll take the scythe and mow it down. Anything to please you!"

"Well, put your garden trousers on, dear," said Mrs. Twiddle. "You don't want to spoil your nice ones."

Twiddle went upstairs and found his garden trousers. They were old, grey flannel ones and he liked them. They were big and comfortable.

He put them on and then took everything out of the pockets of his other trousers and put them into the pockets of his garden trousers. In went his money, his keys, his handkerchief and a little roll of string that he always kept in case he might want some.

Then he went downstairs to find the scythe. "It may be blunt, of course," he said to Mrs. Twiddle. "Then I couldn't start mowing the grass to-day."

"Well, it isn't blunt," said Mrs. Twiddle. "I had it sharpened last week for you. Now do get to work, Twiddle—you've been ages already getting your garden trousers on."

Twiddle went out into the garden. It was rather hot. Oh dear, scything was very very hard work! He would soon be dreadfully hot! He took off his coat.

He walked to the long grass with the big scythe in his hand. Dear, dear, it certainly was very long! He felt the blade of the scythe to see if it really was sharp, and it was.

Now, just as Mr. Twiddle was about to begin his work, the cat walked over to him, and rubbed against his leg in a very loving manner. Twiddle was not very fond of his wife's cat. It always wanted doors or windows opened for it whenever Twiddle was sitting down reading his paper.

"Go away, Puss!" he said, sternly. "I'm going to do a bit of scything. You don't want your tail cut off, do you? Well, use your brains, then, and get away. Shoo!"

The cat rubbed itself against Mr. Twiddle's other leg. Then it sat down and began to wash itself.

"Did you hear what I said?" asked Twiddle. "Go away from this long grass. Right away. Surely you would not be silly enough to lie down and sleep in it just when I'm going to scythe it? Of course, I know that's just the kind of thing you *would* do!"

The cat immediately curled itself up in the grass and tucked its head into its paws. Twiddle stirred it with his foot.

"Now, what did I say? Go and find Mrs. Twiddle! Go along!"

The cat uncurled itself, went a little way away, gave Twiddle a nasty look and settled down again. Mr. Twiddle began to get angry. He ran at the cat.

"Shoo! Get away! Why do you always make things difficult for me?"

The cat decided that Twiddle wanted to have a game with it. It jumped up, crouched down, and ran at Twiddle's feet. Then it darted away into the grass and hid. Twiddle ran at it again. "Shoo! *Will* you go away and let me get on with my work?"

Mrs. Twiddle put her head out of the window. "Twiddle! What *are* you doing rushing about in the grass all by yourself and shouting like that?"

"I'm *not* all by myself!" shouted back Twiddle, indignantly. "The cat's here. How can I cut the grass if she's darting about the whole time?"

He chased the cat all about the grass and at last it ran off to Mrs. Twiddle, its tail straight up in the air. Twiddle, feeling very hot, panted a bit, and then lifted the scythe.

But just as he was about to begin his work he saw something lying in the grass, something bright and round. He picked it up. A sixpence! Well, that was a nice little find. Very nice, indeed. He put it into his pocket with his other money.

"It's a pity I can't find a bit more money," he

said to himself. "If I could I'd pay a man to do this heavy scything."

He cut a piece of grass—and then he suddenly saw something shining once more. He bent down —goodness gracious, it was a shilling!

"Very strange!" said Mr. Twiddle. "Someone's been walking in this grass, I suppose, and dropped a bit of money. Who's been trespassing in my garden? Well, it serves him right to lose his money!"

He lifted his scythe again, and then thought that he might as well have a look to see if there was any more money lying in the long grass. So he put down his scythe and began to look.

He soon saw a penny and a ha'penny! Then he found another sixpence. Well, well, this *was* a nice surprise, to be sure! "Two shillings and a penny ha'penny altogether. Splendid!"

He began to look very carefully indeed, bending down and peering in the grass, parting the long blades hopefully.

"Another shilling! Well, I never! And here's half a crown. Would you believe it! Why, this bit of grass is full of money!"

It was most extraordinary. He kept on picking up pennies and ha'pennies, sixpences and shillings wherever he looked. He put them all into his pocket, feeling very pleased indeed. "I shall get a man to come and do the scything now. Why, I must have picked up about a pound's worth of money already. Very nice, very nice indeed!"

Mrs. Twiddle looked out of the window again to see if Twiddle was getting on well with his scything. She saw him bending down, creeping here and there, then suddenly standing up to put something into his pocket, then bending down again and creeping about. What *was* he doing?

"Twiddle!" shouted Mrs. Twiddle. "What *do* you think you're doing? Surely you're not playing with the cat?"

"I am *not*!" said Twiddle, standing up, looking rather hot. "I'm picking up money."

"Good gracious!" said Mrs. Twiddle. "Money! Whatever do you mean?"

"What I say," said Twiddle, and bent down to pick up a sixpence. He held it up to show her. "It's easy. I just look for it and I see it. It's all over this piece of grass. Wherever I go I find pennies and ha'pennies and sixpences and shillings and half-crowns. Why, here's half a crown by my foot now!"

So there was. Mrs. Twiddle hurried down to the patch of long grass. "Really, Twiddle! I can't believe it. How could there be so much money in this grass? Where in the world did it come from?"

"Somebody must have dropped it," said

Twiddle. "Somebody trespassing in my garden. Serves him right to lose it."

He picked up a sixpence and put it into his pocket. "I'm going to pay a man to do this scything instead of me," he said. "And if you'd like to buy yourself a box of chocolates, wife, I'd be pleased to give you the money. And we might perhaps buy a chicken for our dinner."

Mrs. Twiddle looked very puzzled. She couldn't understand this money business at all. Twiddle wandered away a little and then picked up a penny. "See! I tell you wherever I go in this grass I pick up money."

"Your pocket must be absolutely full of it!" said Mrs. Twiddle. "How much have you got?"

"Well, I've picked up dozens and dozens of pennies and sixpences and shillings and things," said Twiddle. "I'll show you what I've got."

He put his hand into his pocket to get out all the money he had put there. He felt round his pocket and a frown came on his face.

"What's the matter?" said Mrs. Twiddle.

"Most extraordinary thing," said Twiddle,

looking astonished, "I can't feel even a *penny* in my pocket! And yet I put dozens of coins there. Where have they all gone?"

"Let *me* feel," said Mrs. Twiddle, and she put her hand into his pocket. She felt around—and then she found a big hole at the bottom!

"Twiddle! You've got an enormous hole in that pocket. I really do think you are the very stupidest man I've ever known! Here you go walking about with a hole in your pocket, dropping all your money out, and picking it up and putting it in your pocket again and then out it falls, and you pick it up all over again—and think you're so rich we can have chicken for dinner!"

Mr. Twiddle stared at his wife in dismay. He felt the hole in his pocket. "Have I—have I been picking up the same penny and the same sixpence, and the same shilling all the time?" he said. "Wasn't this grass full of money, then?"

"No, you stupid man! Whatever money was here fell from your pocket—when you were chasing the cat about, I should think," said Mrs. Twiddle. "And you kept on picking it up and losing it and picking it up . . . oh, Twiddle, I think my cat's got more sense in its head than you have. Wasting all the morning doing a silly thing like that!"

Twiddle was very upset. He picked up a shilling by his foot and absent-mindedly put it into his pocket. It at once fell out and appeared by his foot again.

"See! That's what's been happening all the time," said Mrs. Twiddle. "Now, you listen to me, Twiddle—I shan't give you any dinner at all till you've finished cutting this grass. So, if you want to play with the cat or go on picking up your money, you know what to expect!"

And little Mrs. Twiddle walked back to the house quite crossly. Twiddle sighed loudly, took his scythe and set to work.

What a disappointment—and how cross Mrs. Twiddle looked. Then a thought came into Twiddle's head. He threw down his scythe and ran across the garden till he came to the kitchen window. He popped his head in and made Mrs. Twiddle jump.

"Now, you listen to me," said Twiddle, quite
fiercely. "Do you know whose fault all this is?
Yours, wife, yours! And do you know why?
Because you didn't mend the hole in my pocket!
Aha! Aha!"

WRT—C

Then, feeling quite pleased with himself, Twiddle went happily back to the grass and scythed hard till it was all cut. And you will be glad to know that Mrs. Twiddle had a lovely dinner ready for him, and gave him a hearty kiss when he came in.

"You're a dear old thing, even if you *are* a stupid!" she said. "Now, don't you dare to say Aha! to me again, or I shall laugh till I cry. Aha, indeed!"

6

A Knot in Twiddle's Hanky

"I DO wish I could remember things," said Mr. Twiddle in despair. "I meant to go and fetch my shoes before the shops closed, so that I could go for a nice walk this evening—and I forgot."

"And you can't possibly go for a walk in those old shoes you're wearing," said Mrs. Twiddle. "Why don't you tie a knot in your hanky, or something, Twiddle, then you would see it and remember you had to do something?"

"Well, that's just what I *will* do!" said Mr. Twiddle, and he took out his big red handkerchief and tied a large knot at one corner. "There! Now, when I see that knot I shall know I must remember something."

"What are you going to remember?" asked Mrs. Twiddle, with a little squeal of laughter.

"Oh, dear me, yes—I forgot I had to have something to remember, before I tied a knot," said Mr. Twiddle. "Well, I know—I really must remember to fetch my shoes to-morrow. I'll leave the knot in for that."

So he left it in, and went to read his paper in the garden. Before very long he took out his red hanky to mop his head—and he saw the knot.

"Aha! The knot! Now that was to make sure I remembered something. What was it?"

But for the life of him poor Mr. Twiddle couldn't remember what the knot was for! So he called his wife. "Wife, can you think of anything I said I would do, and haven't done?" he asked.

"Good gracious, yes!" said Mrs. Twiddle at once, thinking of a whole lot of things. "What about cutting the grass?"

"Oh, dear—did I really put the knot in my hanky for that?" said Mr. Twiddle, with a sigh. "Well, well—it's no good putting knots in if I don't take any notice of them." So he got up, fetched the mowing machine and began to cut the grass.

He was so hot when he had finished that he sat down on the seat to rest. He pulled out his hanky —and in it he saw the knot again. He had forgotten to undo it! So he thought it was another knot, of course. He stared at it, frowning.

"Good gracious! Now what's *this* knot for?" he wondered. He called to his wife. "Is there anything else I ought to do?"

"Dear me, yes! What about weeding the lettuces?" called back his wife, giggling to herself to think that dear old Twiddle hadn't undone the knot.

Twiddle got up. "Well, I never! Was that what the knot was for in my hanky? What a memory I've got, to be sure."

So off he went to weed the lettuce bed, and it took him till supper-time. He was really very tired when he went in.

After his supper he took out his hanky to wipe some crumbs off his waistcoat—and again he saw the very same knot.

"Look at that!" he said to his wife, who turned away to laugh all by herself. "What's *that* knot for, I'd like to know?"

"You haven't filled the coke bucket for me," said Mrs. Twiddle. "Would it be that, Twiddle?"

"It might be," said Twiddle. "Anyway, I'll do it. Oh, dear, what a pity I saw the knot!"

He saw it again just before he went to bed. "Bless us all! Here's a knot in my hanky again!" he said to his wife. "The things I have to remember! What can it be now? Is there anything important I must do?"

"Yes. Put the cat out, and then get her in again," said Mrs. Twiddle, lighting her candle to go up to bed. "You always forget that, Twiddle."

Twiddle groaned. "That cat! I let her in and out all day long. She just does it on purpose. And yet at night, when I kindly open the door for her without her asking me, she won't go out. Puss, come along! Out you go!"

Mrs. Twiddle had gone upstairs by the time Mr. Twiddle had let the cat out and waited patiently for it to come back again. He went up with his candle and got into bed beside his plump little wife.

He took his hanky to put under the pillow—and dear me, he saw the knot again! Yes, the very same knot!

Mrs. Twiddle was asleep. Twiddle couldn't bear to waken her. He stared at the knot and tried to puzzle out what it was there to remind him of. To fasten all the windows? To rake out the kitchen fire? To see if the larder door was safely shut? To—to—to—well, what *was* the knot for?

Poor Twiddle got out of bed, put on his dressing-gown and went downstairs to see if he could find something he had forgotten to do. But he couldn't. The doors were locked, the windows were fastened, the larder was shut, the fire was raked out. Then what could it be?

He went into the sitting-room to see if everything was all right there, and fell over the cat, which got between his legs in her usual annoying way. He fell down with a crash, knocked over a little table, and down went Mrs. Twiddle's pet fern!

Mrs. Twiddle woke up with a dreadful jump. "Twiddle!" she said sharply. "Burglars! Quick, Twiddle!"

But Twiddle wasn't there. Mrs. Twiddle put on her dressing-gown and went downstairs in time to see Twiddle pelting the cat with the earth out of her plant pot! She was very cross indeed.

"Really, Twiddle! Have you *got* to do this sort of thing in the middle of the night when I'm sound asleep? The poor cat! And my poor fern! Puss, Puss, come to me, then. Naughty Twiddle, what was he doing to you?"

"*Well!*" said Twiddle, annoyed. "I like *that*! Why don't you ask your cat what she was doing to *me*? Tripping me up on purpose!"

"What did you come down for?" asked Mrs. Twiddle, crossly.

"Well—to see if I'd forgotten to do something," said Twiddle. "But everything seems all right. I'm coming to bed. But that cat isn't, wife. Leave her in the kitchen, please."

"Poor Pussy!" said Mrs. Twiddle, and put the cat down. They went up to bed together and took off their dressing-gowns. Just as he got into bed Twiddle saw his hanky on the pillow and stared at the knot.

"That knot again!" he cried. "What's it to remind me of *now*, I'd like to know. I'll never put another knot in my hanky again!"

"You won't need to!" said Mrs. Twiddle, with a laugh. "You seem to keep the same one in all the time. You never undo it! Oh, Twiddle, you'll be the death of me one day, with your foolish ways. Now, you listen to me—that knot is to tell you to lie down, shut your eyes and go to sleep!"

"Is it really?" said Twiddle, blowing out his candle and lying down very thankfully. "Well, well, well—to think I put a knot in my hanky to remind me to do something I could *never* forget to do!"

And off he went to sleep. But I wonder if he'll remember to fetch his shoes next day? Do you think he will?

7
Mr. Twiddle Goes Shopping

"TWIDDLE, you are not listening to anything I'm saying!" said Mrs. Twiddle, crossly. "There you sit in your chair, reading your newspaper and not paying any attention to me at all."

"But you were only talking about your shopping, my love," said Mr. Twiddle.

"I know—but *you* are to do the shopping for me to-day, so I want you to listen!" scolded Mrs. Twiddle.

"Aren't you going to make me out a list?" said Mr. Twiddle. "You always take a list yourself."

"Yes, of course I shall make you a list—but you must listen to me all the same," said Mrs. Twiddle.

"Very well, my dear," said Mr. Twiddle, but he didn't listen. He went on reading his paper, and all that Mrs. Twiddle said went in at one ear and out at the other.

Somebody came to the door and Mrs. Twiddle went to open it. When she came back, she had Twiddle's hat and coat and scarf in her hands.

"Here you are, Twiddle," she said. "Put these on and go quickly, or everything in the shops will be sold. Hurry!"

"You always want things done in such a hurry," grumbled Twiddle, putting down his paper and getting up.

He put on his coat and hat and Mrs. Twiddle tied his scarf round his neck. Then she gave him a kiss. "There you are, grumbler. And here is your shopping list. Take the basket and be sure to bring me back everything on the list."

Twiddle put the list in his pocket, picked up the basket, fell over the cat, and went out. It was a nice, bright, frosty day. Twiddle walked fast because it was cold.

He looked at his list. "Butter, Soles, Drops, Corn, Hooks, Cake," he read. "Well, butter is easy. I'll call at the grocer's for that straight away."

He collected the butter. "Soles," he thought. "Good gracious! Does Mrs. Twiddle want soles for her shoes—or soles to eat? Goodness knows!"

He thought the best thing to do would be to buy

a pair of soles at the fish shop, and a pair of soles at the shoe shop. Then whatever happened, he would be right. So that is what he did! Into his basket went the fish, also the soles to go inside slippers.

He looked at the list again. "Drops! Goodness gracious, what kind of drops? Snowdrops? Peppermint drops? Eye drops? Which did Mrs. Twiddle say?"

Well, of course, as Twiddle hadn't listened at all to what Mrs. Twiddle said to him he had no idea which to buy. He decided to get some more eye drops at the chemist's. Mrs. Twiddle had weak eyes and she sometimes put drops into them at night. She might have meant those.

On the other hand she might have meant peppermint drops, which she liked very much. Very well, Mr. Twiddle would get those too! So he went to the sweet shop and bought sixpenny-worth of peppermint drops.

Then he suddenly saw a woman selling bunches of snowdrops at the kerb. Snow*drops*! Well, well—Mrs. Twiddle *might* have meant those.

So he bought a little bunch and put it into his basket.

What was next on the list? Corn? Ah, corn, that was easy. But wait a minute—did Mrs. Twiddle want corn for her hens, or a corn-cure for that big corn she was always complaining about? Twiddle decided to buy both, then Mrs. Twiddle couldn't possibly grumble at him.

So he bought a bag of corn, which was very heavy, and a bottle of corn-cure. What next?

"Hooks. Hooks! Gracious, what kind of hooks? Hooks and eyes—curtain hooks—or crochet hooks?" wondered poor Mr. Twiddle. "Can't be curtain hooks, because she isn't hanging up any curtains. It must be crochet hooks—or hooks and eyes. I'll buy both and after that I'll buy the cake."

It was a very, very heavy basket that Mr. Twiddle took home. He decided to ask Mrs. Twiddle to read down the list to him, and then he would hand out the things she said—perhaps she would add a little explanation as she read them. She might say "soles for our supper," then he would know that meant the fish, and not the slipper-soles, and he could hand out the right thing.

"Hallo, Twiddle dear, what a long time you've been!" said Mrs. Twiddle, when he went into the house. "Have you got everything? I do hope you have. They were all most important."

Mr. Twiddle hoped he had got them too. Mrs. Twiddle wouldn't be at all pleased if he had brought the wrong things!

"Read down the list, dear, and I'll hand out the things," said Twiddle. Mrs. Twiddle took the list and began to read. "Butter, Twiddle—did you get it?"

"Here it is," said Twiddle, and handed it out. "Next, please?"

"Soles, Twiddle. I do hope the fishmonger hadn't sold out," said Mrs. Twiddle. That was a most helpful remark. Mr. Twiddle at once handed out the fish.

"The drops," said Mrs. Twiddle. "Had the chemist got them?"

"Ah," thought Twiddle, as he handed out the eye drops, "this is fine! What a good idea of mine to get Mrs. Twiddle to read out the list!"

"Corn," said Mrs. Twiddle. "Ah, there it is in that bag. What a lovely lot you've brought, Twiddle! The hens *will* enjoy themselves!"

"Easier and easier!" thought Twiddle, feeling very pleased. "What's next, wife?"

"Hooks," said Mrs. Twiddle. "Did you get them?"

Ah—now Twiddle didn't know which hooks

to hand out—the hooks and eyes—or the crochet
hooks! He pretended to stop and think whether
he had got them or not.

"Oh, don't say you forgot my hooks and eyes!"
said Mrs. Twiddle. "I *told* you I wanted to sew
them on to my new dress to-night. Oh, Twiddle!"

"Yes, yes, I got them!" said Twiddle delighted,
and handed out the little packet. "And here's the
cake. That was the last thing on the list, wasn't
it?"

"How clever you are!" said Mrs. Twiddle. She
looked at the basket. "Why, you've got lots more
things there, Twiddle? Snowdrops! How lovely!
Are they for me?"

"Yes," said Twiddle, beaming. "Of course."

"Oh, how kind you are. And what are these?"
said Mrs. Twiddle, opening a bag. "*Pepper*mint
drops! How did you guess I had none left? And,
oh, Twiddle, you don't mean to tell me you
remembered to buy a pair of soles to put in my old
bedroom slippers! How wonderful!"

"Well," began Twiddle, "you see . . ."

But Mrs. Twiddle cut him short and gave him a

hug. "Thank you, thank you," she said. "They're lovely and just the right size."

She dived into the basket again. "Oh, Twiddle, you've bought me a new corn-cure for my poor corn—and you've got some new crochet hooks for me, too. You are really very kind and generous!"

Twiddle felt so pleased. He had done better than he thought! Mrs. Twiddle flew round him; and found his slippers and his pipe. She gave him his newspaper, and made up the fire.

"Now you sit down and have a good read!" she said. "And I'll make you toast and dripping for your tea. You deserve a treat, you nice, kind man!"

Well, he did really, didn't he—and how he enjoyed it!

8

Mr. Twiddle and the Shears

"TWIDDLE!" called Mrs. Twiddle. "Are you going down into the town to-day?"

Twiddle put down his newspaper and groaned. He knew what that question meant. It meant that Mrs. Twiddle had a whole lot of shopping for him to do. But for once in a way he was mistaken. She didn't want any shopping done, she only wanted something taken to be sharpened.

"It's the garden shears," she said. "They are so very blunt that I can't cut the edges of the grass with them. Could you take them to be mended?"

Well, as the shop that mended such things as shears stood just beside the river, where Mr. Twiddle loved to watch the passing ships, he was quite pleased to go. "Yes, I'll go down into the town, now," he said. "If I go now I can watch the twelve o'clock steamer passing under the bridge."

He was very pleased about that. He liked watching the steamer, especially when it was crammed full of people. They all waved to him and that made Twiddle feel very important.

He folded up his paper, put it in his chair ready for when he came home, and went to get his hat and stick. He set off happily.

It was almost twelve o'clock when he got to the bridge. There came the steamer, flags flying, and a band playing—lovely!

Everyone waved to Mr. Twiddle and he waved back happily with his hat. Really, he might be a king, the way he felt when he saw hundreds of people waving like that!

The steamer passed by. Mr. Twiddle put on his hat again and went into the ironmonger's shop. "Yes, sir? What can I do for you?" asked the boy behind the counter.

"I want some garden shears mended," said Mr. Twiddle.

"Shall we fetch them, sir?" asked the boy.

"No, I've . . ." began Mr. Twiddle, and then he stopped. Dear me—where were the shears? He hadn't got them with him! What had he done with them?

"Er—I must have left them somewhere," said Twiddle, and hurried out of the shop. Yes—he had left them at home! He rushed back, and Mrs. Twiddle met him at the door.

"You're in nice time for your dinner, Twiddle," she said, pleased. "When did they say they would have the shears mended? To-day?"

"Well, er—you see—the fact is, I didn't take them," said Twiddle, going rather red. "I quite forgot them, wife. There they are, on the hall-table."

"Really, Twiddle! You do some silly things, I know—but fancy going off to ask for shears to be mended, and leaving them behind all the time!" said Mrs. Twiddle, vexed. "It's too bad of you."

"Yes, it is," said Twiddle. "I'll take them this afternoon."

So, after he had had his dinner, he got his hat and his stick. "Mind you take the shears, too!" said Mrs. Twiddle, calling from the kitchen.

"I've got them under my arm," said Twiddle. "Don't worry!"

Off he went with the shears. It was a lovely day

and soon he overtook his old friend Mr. Wander. Mr. Wander was a great walker, and knew all the little highways and byways of the countryside.

"Where are you going?" he asked Twiddle.

"Nowhere particular," said Twiddle. "Just taking these shears along, that's all. I'll come with you a little way, it's such a nice afternoon."

Well, Twiddle and Wander talked and walked and really enjoyed each other's company. When at last Twiddle found himself back at his front gate, he beamed at Wander and shook him warmly by the hand. "It's a long time since I enjoyed a walk and a talk so much!" he said, and indoors he went.

Mrs. Twiddle came to meet him. "Oh, Twiddle—how lovely! You've waited for the shears to be sharpened and brought them home for me. That *is* nice of you!"

Twiddle stared down at the shears in horror. Gracious! He had carried them all the way there and back and hadn't even gone into the shop! They were as blunt as when he had set off with them.

It was very, very difficult to explain this to Mrs.

Twiddle. She kept saying, "But how *could* you carry the shears under your arm all that way and never once think of getting them sharpened?" Mr. Twiddle felt very foolish and could hardly eat any tea at all.

"Now, to-morrow morning you're to go straight to the shop with those shears, and you're to wait there till they're done," said Mrs. Twiddle. "First you go without them, then you take them all the way there and back and don't have them sharpened—now you just see that you wait for them!"

So the next morning poor Twiddle had no time to read his paper. He had to set off at once with the shears. Oh dear—suppose the shop couldn't do them till the afternoon? What about his dinner? He would have to go without it if he waited for the shears!

He arrived safely at the shop and was glad to see that the shears were still under his arm. Good! Now to ask the boy when they could be done.

"Yes? Brought the shears this time, I see," said the boy with a grin. "You want them sharpened, I suppose, sir?"

"Yes, please," said Twiddle. "When can you do them? I'm—er—well, I'm in a bit of a hurry."

"Can't do them before two o'clock, sir," said the boy, looking at a list of work to be done. "Very sorry."

Mr. Twiddle groaned. He would certainly not get home for dinner, then, because he had promised his wife to wait for the shears. "All right," he said. "I'll wait for them."

He sat down in the shop, and wished he hadn't left his newspaper at home. Then, after a while, he remembered that the eleven o'clock steamer would soon be along. He cheered up a bit. He could go and watch that, and the twelve o'clock one, too— *and* the one o'clock—yes, and he could see the two o'clock one go by as well, just before he collected the shears. Well, well, it wasn't often that he had the chance of watching four steamers in one day.

He went off to wait for the eleven o'clock steamer. He sat in the sun and snoozed, and most unfortunately missed the steamer when it went by. Never mind, he could see the twelve o'clock.

He did, and everyone waved like mad again. Mr. Twiddle waved back so madly that he almost dropped his hat in the water.

At half-past twelve he began to feel very hungry. He considered what to do. He couldn't go home to his dinner because Mrs. Twiddle would be very angry to see him coming home again without the shears. But, if he had enough money in his pocket, he could go and have a nice dinner in the little inn near-by, the one that faced on to the river.

"Then I can watch the boats go by all the time," he thought happily. "Really, this day is turning out to be quite a nice one for me, after all."

He went to the shop to find out how much the shears would be when they were sharpened. Then he would know how much money he would be able to spend on his dinner. The boy was still there, behind the counter.

"Your shears aren't ready yet, sir," he said. "I said two o'clock, you know."

"Yes, I know," said Mr. Twiddle. "I just came in to find out how much they will be when they are done."

"Two shillings and sixpence, sir," said the boy.

"Thank you," said Twiddle. "I'll be in at two o'clock to fetch them. I may as well pay for them now, then I can just take the shears and go, when I come in after dinner."

He paid the two shillings and sixpence and went out. Now he could spend the rest of his money on his dinner. He had four shillings and sixpence. He could get a nice meal at the inn for that.

He watched the one o'clock steamer go by and then went to get his dinner. It was lovely to sit in the window of the inn, eating cold meat and salad, and be able to watch the ships and barges go by at the same time.

He waited for the two o'clock steamer to pass, and then he paid his bill, and walked back to the ironmonger's shop. He went in.

There was nobody there! The boy was lazy and never came back from his dinner at the right time. Bother him!

Twiddle saw a long parcel lying at one end of the counter. It had a ticket on it. Twiddle looked at it, feeling sure that it was his shears. The ticket said 2s. 6d.

"Half a crown—yes, this is my parcel," he said, pleased. "Well, as I've paid the bill I don't see why I can't collect these shears and go. It's not my fault that the boy is so late back from his dinner."

So he put the parcel under his arm and off he went. Mrs. Twiddle was out in the garden, trying to cut the grass-edges with an old pair of shears. She was very pleased to see him.

"Ah, good!" she said. "You've brought them back at last—sharpened this time, I hope! How much were they?"

"Two and six," said Twiddle, and Mrs. Twiddle tut-tutted and said that was a dreadful price. She tore the paper off—and then gave a scream.

"Twiddle! What's this? It's a saw! A *saw*! Do you mean to tell me you took our saw to be

sharpened instead of the shears? Well, really,
REALLY! I don't know what to say to you,
honestly I don't."

All the same, she said a lot, and Twiddle had to
listen. He was puzzled. *Had* he taken the saw
instead of the sheats? No—he knew he hadn't.
Then he had taken somebody else's parcel instead
of his own. What a tiresome nuisance.

"Oh—so that's the next silly thing you did, is
it?" said Mrs. Twiddle. "Well, I'll give you one
more chance of being silly—you can just take this
saw back to the shop straight away and get the
shears instead!"

So off went poor Mr. Twiddle once more. He
came to the shop and told the boy what had
happened.

"I've brought back the saw, so can I take my
shears now?" he asked.

"Oh, my!" said the boy. "I must have given
them to the other customer, when he came for his
saw. They were wrapped up, too, you see. He lives
at Romer Green, five miles away."

Well, well, well!—that was too much for Mr.

Twiddle altogether. He looked desperately round the shop. He saw a pair of brand-new shears hanging there.

"I'll buy these," he said. "Give them to me now. I'll come in and pay for them to-morrow."

And he went off home with a new pair of shears for Mrs. Twiddle—but whether she'll be pleased or not about that I really don't know. Twiddle **does** really do some peculiar things, doesn't he?

9
Mr. Twiddle's Shadow

MR. TWIDDLE was very angry with the cat. He spoke to it very sternly indeed.

"Now you listen to me, Cat! You have a good home here and plenty to eat, and a nice basket of your own. And what do you do? You steal things out of the larder if the door is left open so much as a crack, and you . . ."

The cat turned its back on Mr. Twiddle and began to wash itself, wetting its paws and rubbing them over its face.

"Turn round!" said Mr. Twiddle, in a rage. "Don't you know your manners? I'm talking to you. Stop doing that soap-and-flannel act of yours, washing your silly face over and over, and look at me!"

The cat didn't. It just went on washing itself. Twiddle marched round to the other side of it and addressed it again.

"All right! If you think you can turn your back on me, you're wrong. Now, just let me tell you

the things you've done to annoy me to-day. I left
the breakfast table for just one moment and what
did you do? Jumped up and ate all my bacon. And
you . . ."

The cat turned its back to Twiddle again and
began to wash another bit of itself. Twiddle flew
into a real temper and stamped his foot. He began
to shout.

"Rude creature! You stole my bacon, you made
me open the window twice—once for you to come
in and once for you to go out—and you tripped
me up in the passage when I was carrying the
milk. You did it on purpose so that you could lick
up the milk!"

The cat walked haughtily to the door, stood by
it, miaowed, and looked round at Twiddle.

"Ha! Now you're ordering me to open the door,
are you?" said Twiddle. "Well, I won't. I've had
enough of you, see? I shall not open another
window or door for you all my life long!"

The cat sat down patiently by the door and
began to wash itself again. Twiddle went on
muttering. The kettle began to boil on the stove.

Twiddle ran to take it off before it dripped all over the place.

The cat ran, too, and tripped up Twiddle as neatly as could be.

Down he went with the kettle and a tiny drop of the scalding water went over the cat. She set up such a hullabaloo that Mrs. Twiddle came rushing into the kitchen.

She was just in time to see Twiddle give the cat a most resounding whack. She was horrified.

"TWIDDLE! What are you doing to MY cat? I saw you smack it—and oh, poor thing, it must have got its tail scalded by the hot water!"

"It's been licking itself all morning," said Twiddle. "What about *me*? I've scalded myself, too—look, on my hand. That cat tripped me up on purpose to make me spill the water. Yes, I smacked it—and if it sits and looks at me like that I'll smack it again!"

"TWIDDLE!" cried Mrs. Twiddle, amazed. "This isn't like you. You sound so hard and horrid."

"I *feel* hard and horrid," said poor Twiddle, holding his scalded hand. "I hope I've done the cat a lot of good, giving her a good smack like that. For two pins I'd give her another."

"Now, stop, Twiddle," said his wife, getting very stern. "It doesn't do her any good to smack her."

"How do you know?" said Twiddle. "You've never smacked her. I tell you smacking is what she wants. I tell you smacking will make a different cat of her."

"Well, it won't," said Mrs. Twiddle. "It will just make her hate and hate you, Twiddle. You're very unkind indeed. That poor cat will never go near you again."

"Well, that will be a very good thing," said Twiddle. "All the same I still say that smack has done her good."

Mrs. Twiddle was cross with him. She put on what Twiddle called her "haughty face" and he didn't like it a bit. "She keeps looking at me as if I was something on the rubbish heap," he grumbled to himself. "Oh dear, how long is she going to keep this up? It will make me miserable."

The cat didn't go near Twiddle. It kept round Mrs. Twiddle and mewed pitifully. Twiddle knew it was just making a fuss. Mrs. Twiddle gave it all kinds of tit-bits and petted it and fussed it till poor Twiddle nearly went mad. Had that smack done it any good after all? If only it had!

Mrs. Twiddle was so cold to poor Twiddle all day long that he really couldn't bear it. He very nearly said he was sorry he had been unkind to the cat, and only just stopped himself in time.

Then an idea came to him. It was a very silly idea, but still it *was* an idea. Mr. Twiddle put on his coat and hat and called to his wife.

"Just going to get an evening paper, wife!"

And off he went. He bought the paper and then he went to the fishmonger's, where he bought a pound of yesterday's fish. It wasn't very fresh and the fishmonger was rather surprised at Twiddle picking out stale fish. Still, he didn't mind selling it, so off went Twiddle, the fish under his arm.

When he got to the field not far from his home, Mr. Twiddle began to act in a most peculiar manner. He stepped into the field, looked cautiously round to make sure no one was watching him, and undid the parcel of stale fish. He spread it on the grass and then stamped on it! How he stamped! He jumped up and down on it too, and he even wiped the fish paper round his boots.

"There!" said Twiddle, walking out of the field and leaving the stale, jumped-on fish behind.

"Now if that cat doesn't follow me round like a shadow all this evening I shall be very surprised! Ha! Mrs. Twiddle said the cat would never come near me again—but she will!"

He went in at the back door. Mrs. Twiddle was in the kitchen, sweeping up some crumbs. The cat was sitting haughtily in the scullery. It gave Twiddle a very nasty look.

Twiddle walked in boldly, and pretended to aim a kick at the cat. It caught a whiff of the fishy smell on his boots, and opened its eyes wide. It sat up straight. My, what a wonderful smell!

Twiddle walked through into the kitchen. The cat followed at once, sniffing eagerly. It came right to Twiddle's heels. Mrs. Twiddle looked up, still with her "haughty face." She was surprised to see the cat following Twiddle so closely.

"Nice and cosy in here, wife," said Twiddle, amiably. "I'll just hang my things in the hall."

He went into the hall. The cat followed closely at his heels and came back at his heels, too, feeling excited. Twiddle had never smelt so nice before. Where *had* he been, thought the cat.

Twiddle walked through the kitchen and into the scullery, just to let his wife see the cat following him again. Mrs. Twiddle said nothing, but she couldn't help feeling more and more astonished. She knew her cat. It was a touchy cat. Even a cross word made it sulk, and it never had liked Mr. Twiddle, who was very free with his cross words at times.

"I'm just going to get the wood in for the morning," said Twiddle, and he walked out into the garden. The cat followed him, almost bumping its nose into his heels.

"Call your cat," said Twiddle, stopping so suddenly that the cat *did* bump its nose. "It's better in the warm kitchen, wife."

"Puss, Puss!" called Mrs. Twiddle. "Come to me, Puss dear."

Puss-dear took not the slightest notice. She began to purr round Twiddle, and even rubbed her head against his legs. Mrs. Twiddle simply couldn't understand it.

"PUSS!" she called sharply. She didn't like the cat not coming to her when it was called. The cat gave her a sour look, and went on purring round Twiddle.

"Oh well, if she wants to be my shadow, let her!" said Twiddle airily, and went to the wood-shed, followed by the cat.

He came back with the cat. He went upstairs and the cat went too. He went to wash his hands in the bathroom and when Mrs. Twiddle popped her head round the door, there was the cat, almost sitting on Twiddle's feet.

Twiddle came into the kitchen with the purring cat. He sat down in his chair. "Now," he said sternly to the cat, "I do *not* want you on my knee. I am still not pleased with you. Just remember that hard smack I gave you this morning, and behave yourself!"

The cat didn't attempt to jump up as she usually did. She sat down contentedly at Twiddle's feet, so that the fishy smell on his boots kept coming to her nose. She suddenly turned her head and began to lick his boots with her pink tongue.

Mrs. Twiddle was ironing and watching all the time. She put down her iron. "Twiddle," she said, in a much nicer voice than she had spoken to him all day, "Twiddle, look at that cat—it's licking your boots!"

"Yes, I know. It's learnt that I'm master at last," said Twiddle comfortably. "I told you that a smack would do it good. It knows it's got to mind its p's and q's with me now. Any more nonsense from it and it will get another smack."

Mrs. Twiddle didn't say a word to that. She was thinking very hard. She had never seen the cat so attached to Twiddle before. Why, Twiddle might be its best friend instead of someone who had scalded it and smacked it not very many hours ago! Could it be that Twiddle was right? Did it need a good smack sometimes?

She went on ironing. The cat licked Twiddle's boots a bit longer, then lay down on his feet and went to sleep.

Mrs. Twiddle simply could not get over its behaviour.

"Twiddle," she said, after a bit, "there's a funny sort of smell in this kitchen, isn't there? Sort of fishy smell."

"Nonsense, my dear!" said Twiddle at once. "Drains, I expect. You're always imagining things."

"I hope the cat hasn't had the fish out of the larder," said Mrs. Twiddle, and she went to look. "If she has I shall give her a good smack!"

That was too much for Mr. Twiddle. He burst into such a loud laugh that the cat nearly jumped out of its skin. "That's right, wife," said Twiddle. "I tell you, this cat is all the better for a good smack!"

He went out to post a letter, later on, not because he wanted to, but because he meant to show Mrs. Twiddle that the cat would even go out to walk with him. It did, of course, keeping to his heels like a shadow again. Mrs. Twiddle was most impressed.

Twiddle sat down again when he got in. "Here

are your slippers, Twiddle, dear," said Mrs. Twiddle, in a meek voice, when he came in. "I've warmed them for you."

Twiddle was about to take them when he remembered not to. It would never do to take off his fishy boots—the cat would desert him at once! "Can't be bothered to put on my slippers," he said, much to Mrs. Twiddle's astonishment. Really, what with Twiddle's behaviour and the cat's, she felt quite bewildered!

"Now, listen, wife. I won't have the cat wandering up into our bedroom to-night," said Twiddle, sternly, when he and his wife were ready to go to bed. "I'm tired of her sleeping on my middle. I can't think why she never sleeps on yours. She must stay down here in the scullery."

"She won't," said Mrs. Twiddle.

"She will," said Twiddle. He took off his boots and took them into the scullery. He stood them by the door to clean them in the morning. Then he spoke sternly to the cat.

"Cat! Sit down there by my boots and don't stir from them all night long. Do you hear?"

"Miaow," said the cat, obediently, and lay down as close to the fishy boots as she possibly could. Mrs. Twiddle could hardly believe her eyes.

"I think you're rather a wonderful man, Twiddle," she said, when they went upstairs. "Honestly, I never saw the cat so well-behaved— why, it was just like your shadow."

"Well, just you be firm with it," said Twiddle. "And mind you back me up when it annoys me.

Next time it trips me up and I smack it, you must smack it, too."

"Oh, I think one smack would be enough," said kind Mrs. Twiddle. "Well, well, to think of that cat adoring you all evening like that! Who would have thought it? I feel quite jealous!"

"Oh, it will stop bothering itself about me to-morrow," said Mr. Twiddle, getting into bed, "and it will follow you around just as usual. You'll see!"

It will, of course, because old Twiddle will have cleaned his boots and they won't smell fishy any more!

The thing is, he sometimes forgets to clean them, and if Mrs. Twiddle happens to do them for him, *what* will she think of the fishy smell? Twiddle, be sure you don't forget!

10

Mrs. Twiddle's Umbrella

"I'm just going out to fetch my paper," Mr. Twiddle called to Mrs. Twiddle. "I won't be long."

"Take your umbrella, then, because it's raining hard," called back Mrs. Twiddle.

Twiddle looked for his umbrella. He couldn't find it anywhere. It wasn't in the hall-stand, it wasn't hanging up with his coat, it wasn't upstairs in his bedroom.

"That tiresome umbrella!" muttered Mr. Twiddle to himself. "It's always disappearing. Could I have left it anywhere, I wonder?"

He thought hard. He might have left it at the post office. He might have left it at the butcher's. He might have left it at the fishmonger's. There were any amount of places where he had already left it at one time or another, and might have left it again the last time it rained.

Twiddle felt guilty. Mrs. Twiddle always had a lot to say when he couldn't find his umbrella.

She would make him go and ask at every shop in the town if she knew it wasn't in the hall-stand.

"Haven't you gone yet?" called Mrs. Twiddle. "Do go, dear. I want you back in good time for dinner, you know. And bring back some fish for the cat, will you?"

"All right," called Twiddle. "Though I don't know why that cat should have so much fish. It has far more than we do. And I do hate carrying fish home on a wet day. It smells so, and——"

"Now, Twiddle, take a basket and go," called Mrs. Twiddle. "Do you want me to come and button your coat and find your hat and put up your umbrella for you? Really, if I don't you'll never get away this morning."

Twiddle looked once more at the hall-stand in despair. Where, oh, where was his tiresome umbrella? He heard Mrs. Twiddle coming, and he snatched at the only umbrella in the stand. It belonged to Mrs. Twiddle. Never mind, he would borrow it just this once.

He rushed out of the front door and banged it behind him. He buttoned his coat and put up his

umbrella as he went down the path, afraid that Mrs. Twiddle might call him back. She would be very cross if she knew he couldn't find his own umbrella and had taken hers.

Mr. Twiddle went to get his paper. He stuffed it into his pocket because he didn't want it to get wet. Then he actually remembered to call at the fish-shop for some fish for the cat. Twiddle didn't like his wife's cat. It always sat just where he could fall over it.

The fishmonger stuffed some fish-heads and fishtails into a bit of paper. Mr. Twiddle took the parcel in disgust. Why hadn't he brought a basket as Mrs. Twiddle had suggested? Now, his hands would smell of fish all day.

He put up his umbrella again and walked off down the street. Somebody called to him: "Hey, Mr. Twiddle! The sun is out and the rain's stopped. Why have you got your umbrella up?"

Twiddle stopped at once, feeling very foolish. Yes, it is a lovely sunny morning now, and he hadn't noticed. He tried to put the umbrella down with one hand, because he had the fish in the other,

but he couldn't. It was too stiff. So he put the fish
on a wall for a moment and then managed to put
the umbrella down.

"Meeow!" said a delighted voice, and a big
tabby cat jumped up beside the fish. It tore at the
bit of paper that wrapped it.

"Stop that!" said Twiddle, crossly, and gave
the cat a whack with his umbrella. It yowled, and
disappeared, taking with it the bit of paper the
fish had been wrapped in.

"Bother!" said Twiddle annoyed. "Now the fish hasn't got any paper—look at all the heads and tails slithering about on the wall. I can't carry them like that."

He remembered his own newspaper safely stuffed in his pocket. He'd have to wrap the fish in that. How horrid! Still, there was nothing else to be done.

Twiddle carefully hooked his wife's umbrella in the branch of a tree that hung down over the wall. He wrapped the fish-scraps in his paper, and walked off down the street.

He left his wife's umbrella behind him, of course. He never once thought of it until the rain suddenly began to fall again. Then he found he hadn't an umbrella to put up!

"Oh, my! I hooked it on to that branch by the wall where I wrapped up the fish in my paper," he groaned, and rushed back to get it.

But it wasn't there. Not a sign of an umbrella could he see! He called out to the woman in the little sweet-shop opposite.

"Did you see anyone take an umbrella from this branch here? I left it not long ago."

"Oh, yes," called back the sweet-shop woman.
"Somebody took it not five minutes ago."

"The thief!" said Twiddle, indignantly. "What
was he like?"

"It wasn't a he, it was a she," said the woman.
"It was somebody dressed in a blue mackintosh
and a hat with daisies on. She was rather plump,
and hurried along like anything."

"Thank you!" called Twiddle. "I'll track down
that nasty woman if it takes me all morning!"

So off he went, hunting for a plump woman in a
blue mackintosh and a hat with daisies on it. He
couldn't see her anywhere. He stopped a man on a
corner and asked him if he had seen anyone
dressed like that.

"Yes," said the man. "She passed me at
the bottom of that road. She was going
towards the bicycle shop, if you know where that
is."

Twiddle did. He raced along to the bicycle shop,
getting wetter and wetter as the rain poured down.
He felt very angry indeed. To think that that thief
of a woman should steal his wife's umbrella and

send him on a goose-chase like this in the pouring rain.

He went into the shop. "Did somebody wearing a blue mackintosh and a hat with daisies on come in here?" he asked. "Somebody with a very nice umbrella—with a dog's head on the crook-handle?"

"Yes," said the boy there. "She did. She said she was going down to the baker's—you might get her there."

Off went Twiddle to the baker's. He peered inside. Nobody there at all. "What do you want?" called the baker's wife.

"Somebody in a blue mackintosh and a hat with daisies," called Twiddle in despair.

"Oh, she came in for a cake just now," said the woman. "She's only just gone. Hurry round the corner and you'll catch her!"

Twiddle hurried—ah, there was somebody in a blue mackintosh and hat with daisies, scurrying along with an umbrella up—his wife's umbrella, too! How dared the woman be such a thief? She deserved to go to prison.

At that very moment Mr. Plod, the policeman, came round a corner and nearly bumped into Twiddle.

"'Morning, Mr. Twiddle," said Mr. Plod. "How wet you are! I thought only policemen had to go out in the rain without umbrellas!"

"Mr. Plod, you're just the man I want," said

Twiddle, eagerly. "Someone's stolen my wife's umbrella, and the thief is there—look, down the road in front of us—with the very umbrella! What shall I do?"

"*I'll* deal with this," said Mr. Plod. "That's what policemen are for. Come along with me, sir."

So Mr. Plod and Mr. Twiddle hurried after the thief in the blue mackintosh. Aha! She would soon be very frightened indeed.

"There—she's gone into Mrs. Chatter's house," said Mr. Plod. "We'll have to go and knock at the door and get in and face her. Come along."

Mr. Plod knocked loudly at the door. Mrs. Chatter opened it and Mr. Plod walked in.

Mr. Twiddle stayed at the front door. He thought he would let Mr. Plod deal with this. He heard the policeman's rumbling voice.

"I've had a report that an umbrella has been stolen," he said. "Was it you, madam, who took it?"

A voice answered him indignantly. "Yes, it *was* me—and why shouldn't I take it? It was my own umbrella! There it was, hanging on the branch of a tree in the middle of the village street—*my* umbrella! I'd like to know who put it there! Just wait till I find out who took my umbrella and hung it on a tree in the village street!"

"Dear me," said Mr. Plod. "Are you *sure* it was your own umbrella? What is your name, madam?"

"You know my name quite well—I'm Mrs. Twiddle!" said the voice indignantly.

Well, Mr. Twiddle could have told Mr. Plod that, of course. He knew his wife's voice very well indeed. He stood shivering at the front door, feeling very upset indeed.

"You wait till Mr. Twiddle hears about this," went on Mrs. Twiddle. "He went out this morning with his own umbrella—and a little later I remembered I had to go out too. But I couldn't find my umbrella at all, so I put on my oldest hat and my mackintosh and out I went without one. And just IMAGINE how astonished I was suddenly to see my very own umbrella hanging on a tree in the village street! I couldn't believe my eyes."

"Very strange," agreed the policeman, wondering what Mr. Twiddle was going to say about all this.

"And now you come banging at my friend's door and tell me somebody says I've stolen my own umbrella!" went on Mrs. Twiddle. "I never heard anything like it. Show me the person who says I stole it, and I'll show you the thief—it must be he who took my umbrella and hung it on that tree! He must be mad. He must be . . ."

Twiddle didn't wait to hear any more. Feeling very sick indeed, he stole off down the path. He hoped Mr. Plod wouldn't give him away. If only he could get home before Mrs. Twiddle discovered anything more!

Mr. Plod didn't give him away. He apologised to Mrs. Twiddle and went off in a hurry before she could ask him any awkward questions. Mrs. Twiddle went home with her umbrella, very cross indeed.

Twiddle had got there first. He had opened the front door and had fallen over the cat, who, as usual, loved to sit in the very middle of the dark hall.

The cat sniffed at him. He smelt very pleasantly of fish. Twiddle felt about for the fish he had bought.

But he hadn't got it. He had left it on the wall when he had gone back to look for the umbrella!

"If you think I'm going back there to look for your fish, you're mistaken, Cat," he said. But then he remembered that his morning paper was round the fish—and he wouldn't be able to read the news if he didn't get the fish!

He groaned and went to the front door again, followed by the excited cat.

He peered out. It was pouring with rain. He stepped out valiantly into it—and bumped into

Mrs. Twiddle hurrying down the path with her umbrella up!

"Twiddle, you're not going out again, are you?" she cried. "I've got such a lot to tell you. Why are you going out again?"

"I've forgotten the cat's fish," said Twiddle, desperately.

"Oh, never mind for once," said Mrs. Twiddle,

anxious to tell Twiddle the story of her umbrella and Mr. Plod.

"I *must* go and get it," said Twiddle and shook himself away from his wife.

"Oh, Twiddle, it's very kind of you, but the cat can go without for once!" cried Mrs. Twiddle. "Come back. Where's your umbrella?"

"I don't know," said Twiddle, in despair.

"But, Twiddle, you went out with your umbrella this morning—I saw you!" cried Mrs. Twiddle. "Oh, Twiddle, have you lost it *again*? Did you come home without it? Here, take mine."

"No, no, NO!" shouted Twiddle, who felt that he could never touch his wife's umbrella again. "I'd rather get soaked!"

And off went poor old Twiddle into the rain to get back the fish and his paper. But the tabby cat had been there before him, so he won't find either. Really, he is a most unlucky fellow, isn't he?

11

When Mr. Twiddle was Asleep

"I DON'T know when I've felt so sleepy," said Mr. Twiddle, yawning, one afternoon.

"You always do feel sleepy in the afternoon," said Mrs. Twiddle, bustling round. "And you always say exactly what you've just said. Now, Twiddle, I'm going out to see old Mrs. Tabbit. You stay here in case anyone comes to the door."

"Right!" said Twiddle, pleased at the idea of a peaceful afternoon in front of the fire. "Is anyone likely to come?"

"No," said Mrs. Twiddle. "And, Twiddle, see that the door is kept shut, will you, so that the cat doesn't get in and wander round. She'll try to get my knitting if she can. She's been a naughty puss lately over that."

"I'll be very pleased to keep the cat out," said Twiddle, settling down in his chair and opening his newspaper. "Nothing I should like better. The longer she's out the more I'll be pleased."

Mrs. Twiddle put on her hat and coat and said

good-bye. "Now have a good snooze," she said. "You really do look rather tired—been reading the newspaper too much, I expect! Good-bye, Twiddle dear."

"Good-bye, my love," said Twiddle, feeling very amiable indeed. Fancy having an afternoon with nobody telling him to do this, that and the other—and the cat forbidden to come in, too! Now she wouldn't be able to sit herself on his knee all the afternoon and dig her claws into him. Aha! this was wonderful.

He was asleep before Mrs. Twiddle had passed by the window. She had a look in and smiled to herself. "Poor old Twiddle—he really *is* tired to-day!" she thought. "I do hope nothing disturbs him."

She went on her way to Mrs. Tabbit's. Half-way there she met Mr. Screw, the carpenter. He nodded to her.

"You naughty man!" said Mrs. Twiddle, playfully. "You haven't been to do the lock of my kitchen door yet—and it *is* so difficult to lock."

"Well, there, ma'am—if I hadn't forgotten all

about it!" said Mr. Screw. He was a great big man, with a shock of red hair and a big nose. "I'm right down sorry. Look, I've got a bit of time this afternoon. I'll go right along and do it now."

"Oh, that *would* be nice of you," said Mrs. Twiddle. "Could you really? The only thing is—

you'll disturb Mr. Twiddle. He's asleep in the kitchen and really very tired."

"He sleeps so soundly that he won't hear *me*," said Mr. Screw. "I'll be very quiet, ma'am. He won't know I've been."

So off he hurried to Twiddle's house. He was soon there. He peeped in at the kitchen window and saw Twiddle fast asleep. He went to the door and opened it.

He examined the lock. Dear, dear, he hadn't got the right tools with him—and if he tried to do it without them he would probably make a tremendous noise, and that would wake up Mr. Twiddle.

Mr. Screw scratched his head. If he went to fetch the right tools, and came back again, he'd be late for his next job. What could he do? Perhaps he had better make a noise after all and chance waking up Mr. Twiddle?

"No, I won't do that," said the carpenter, suddenly. "I know a better idea. I'll simply take the door off its hinges and carry it home with me— do the lock there and carry the door back. It won't take me any time then."

So, very quietly, he began to take the door off its hinges. The cat came and watched him with much interest. She hadn't seen a door taken off before. She was pleased. Now she could get into the warm kitchen and perhaps find something to eat.

"Miaow!" said the cat and rubbed herself against the carpenter.

"Sh!" said the carpenter. "You'll wake Mr. Twiddle."

The cat didn't mind about that at all, and went on miaowing. But Twiddle didn't stir. He was fast asleep and dreaming a wonderful dream about a dish of fried steak and onions that never grew smaller however much he ate of it. He snored a little.

Soon the carpenter had the door right off. He lifted it up on his shoulder and went off with it. The cat shot into the room as soon as the doorway was empty and leapt on to Twiddle's knee, digging her claws into him as usual.

Twiddle woke up with a jump. He stared at the cat in anger. "How did *you* get in?" he asked, exasperated. "Door and window shut and yet you appear. Get down from my knee at once."

"Miaow," said the cat and tried to rub her head against Twiddle's chin. That was too much. He put her down and shut his eyes again. "I don't know how you got in, but you can go out the same way," he said.

An icy draught blew round his chair. Twiddle sat up and looked at the fire. Had it gone down while he was asleep? Why was the room so cold?

No, the fire was beautiful. He sat back again and shut his eyes. But a little wind lifted his hair at the top, where it showed above the chair. Twiddle was puzzled. *Where* was this frightful draught coming from?

He looked round his chair—and to his enormous surprise, he saw the empty doorway. The wind was blowing through and making the place as cold as could be.

Twiddle didn't notice that the door was gone at first—he simply thought it was wide open. He glared at the cat. "Did *you* manage to open that door on your own, you maddening, tiresome cat?"

The cat said nothing but began to wash herself. Twiddle got up and went to shut the door.

But the door, of course, wasn't there. Twiddle stared as if he couldn't believe his eyes. He ran his hand round the doorway—no, there was no door at all. It had absolutely vanished!

"Well—I must still be asleep, that's all," said Twiddle, bewildered. "I'll go and sit down again and maybe the door will be back again when I next wake up."

So he went and sat down again—but he was so puzzled that he couldn't go to sleep. He kept looking round his chair at the empty doorway, and shivering in the draught.

"Somebody must have stolen the door!" he said to himself at last. "A thief must have crept up when I was asleep, and taken the door off—the wicked robber!"

He went into the garden and called his next-door neighbour. "Hey! Did you see a man carrying a door this afternoon?"

The neighbour stared. "No. Why should I? People don't usually go about carrying doors."

"Well, *someone* is going about carrying a door," said Twiddle, suddenly feeling very fierce indeed, "and what's more I'm going to find out who it is!"

He rushed indoors, fell over the cat, got his hat and stick and rushed out. He trotted into the town, looking everywhere for a man carrying a door. But there wasn't one to be seen anywhere. This

wasn't surprising, because the carpenter was now busily mending the lock in his own workroom.

As soon as he had finished it, he popped the door on his shoulder again and off he went back to Mr. Twiddle's house. By that time Twiddle was at the other end of the town, walking up the steps to the police station, looking very fierce indeed.

"What do you want, sir?" asked the constable there.

"Someone's stolen my door!" said Twiddle, and he banged his hand on the desk. "I want it back!"

"What door?" asked the policeman, astonished.

"My kitchen door," said Mr. Twiddle. "When I was fast asleep, too. Taken it right away."

"Er—well—this is very peculiar," said the constable, and reached for his helmet. "I'll come with you and make a report, sir."

Twiddle marched him all the way to his house. He went down the back path to the kitchen door. "This is where the door was stolen," he said, and stopped suddenly.

The door was back! There it was, fast shut,

and looking very solid indeed. Mr. Screw had put it back five minutes before and had then gone off again.

The policeman stared stolidly at the door. "You playing a joke on me?" he enquired.

Mr. Twiddle looked scared. He felt the door gingerly. It was real and solid—but when he had left the house it hadn't been there. Now it was back! He simply couldn't understand it!

"Er—very peculiar," said Mr. Twiddle, still staring at the door. "It wasn't there when I left. Now it's come back."

"Doors don't come and go like that," said the constable, putting away his note-book. "I don't suppose you took a good look, sir—the door must have been there all the time. Good afternoon."

Mrs. Twiddle came in at that moment and was most surprised to see a policeman going out of the back gate. She hurried up to Twiddle, who was still standing outside the back door, looking puzzled.

"Twiddle, what have you been up to? Why did that policeman call?" she panted.

"Well—er—it was nothing much," said Twiddle, suddenly feeling that he didn't really want to discuss vanishing doors with Mrs. Twiddle. He didn't feel that she would believe him. "He—er—well, he just came about a door."

"About a *door*!" said Mrs. Twiddle, even more astonished. "What door?"

She opened the kitchen door and went inside. The very first thing she saw was the cat playing with her knitting! It had rolled the ball of wool all over the place, and had undone half the jumper she was making. Now it was busy chewing her needles!

She gave a scream. "Oh, you wicked cat! Give her a smack, quick, Twiddle!"

Twiddle was only too pleased. He smacked hard at the cat, which dodged aside, and Twiddle hit his hand hard against the dresser. The cat fled out of the open door.

"*You* deserve a smack, too, Twiddle," said Mrs. Twiddle, angrily. "Didn't I *ask* you not to let the cat in?"

"I didn't let her in," said Twiddle, sucking his hand.

"Well, you must have done. She can't come in through a shut door," said Mrs. Twiddle.

"She did," said Twiddle. "But wait a minute—perhaps she didn't. Perhaps she came in after the door had gone!"

"Gone?" said Mrs. Twiddle, staring at Twiddle. "*Gone?* What do you mean—*gone?* Doors don't go."

"This one did," said Twiddle; "I fetched the police about it. And when we came back, the door had come again."

"Twiddle, dear, do you feel quite well?" said Mrs. Twiddle, suddenly, thinking he must be going mad or something. "Would you like to go to bed?"

Twiddle thought it would be a good idea. Then perhaps he wouldn't have to do any more explaining about cats and knitting and doors that came and went.

"I think I *will* go to bed," said Twiddle. So up he went. Mrs. Twiddle fussed over him like anything. She gave him a hot-water bottle, she brought him hot milk, she even went out to buy him a late newspaper. He was tremendously pleased. He really enjoyed himself.

He's never found out why the door came and went, because the carpenter didn't bother to tell Mrs. Twiddle about it. Mr. Twiddle would have forgotten all about it long ago, if it wasn't that he keeps meeting the policeman he fetched that day.

"'Morning, Mr. Twiddle," the policeman says each time. "Had any more trouble with your *doors*?"

Dear old Twiddle! I can't help liking him; can you?

12

Twiddle goes for a Walk

MRS. TWIDDLE bustled in just at teatime. It was a winter's evening, and already almost dark outside. She called Twiddle.

"Twiddle! Twiddle! Where are you? Have you got the tea ready as I told you?"

Twiddle hadn't. He had gone to sleep in front of the kitchen fire, and had only just woken up when he heard Mrs. Twiddle come in. He was now scurrying round filling the kettle, putting it on the stove, and trying to get out all the tea things at once!

"Twiddle! Can't you hear me? I'm home!" called Mrs. Twiddle, walking into the kitchen. "Dear me—you haven't even got the tea laid."

"Just ready, *just* ready!" said Twiddle, banging the loaf down on the platter. "You must be early, my dear."

"No, I'm not!" said Mrs. Twiddle, taking off her hat. "I'm late. And I'm tired and thirsty. I suppose you slept in front of the kitchen fire from the moment I went out and shut the door to the moment I came back, Twiddle. And I suppose you haven't done a single thing I asked you to—not one!"

Twiddle fell over the cat and didn't answer. He glared at the cat. "Did you do that on purpose, you miserable animal? How did you get in? You were outside when I began to get tea."

"Oh, Twiddle—she must have got in through the bedroom window," said Mrs. Twiddle. "And I *asked* you to be sure and shut it if it rained. You can't have shut it. Did you?"

As Twiddle hadn't even known it had been raining that afternoon he certainly hadn't shut the window. Trust that cat to give him away!

"And did you fetch in some more coal as I asked you?" asked Mrs. Twiddle. "Oh, dear—no, you didn't! The scuttle is empty. And did you take the clothes in off the line? Oh, *Twiddle*—they're still there. I can see them flapping in the darkness. They'll be soaked with the rain! And what about the dog? Did you take him for a short walk?"

Twiddle hadn't done anything at all except go to

sleep. He felt very much ashamed of himself. Dear, dear—he hadn't even *thought* about the dog!

"Oh, Twiddle—I do think you are very very mean," said poor Mrs. Twiddle, sitting down. "I've been busy all the afternoon nursing my poor sister, and I did so want my tea ready when I got home. I don't believe you love me one bit. Not one bit. You haven't done a thing I asked you."

To Twiddle's horror she burst into tears. He hurried over with his big hanky, but she pushed him away.

"No! You don't love me!" she sobbed. "I know you don't. You just went to sleep and forgot all about me."

Twiddle felt very guilty indeed. He felt lazy and unkind and selfish and good-for-nothing. He tried again to dry his wife's eyes. But she wouldn't let him. Twiddle was very miserable.

What could he do to put things right? He rushed about, made the tea, cut bread and butter and put out cakes. He tore out into the darkness and brought in the clothes from the line. He fell over the cat again, and didn't say a word. He rushed upstairs and shut the bedroom window, because it was raining once more. He went out and got some more coal in. The cat went with him, very interested in Twiddle's sudden fit of hurry-scurry.

He nearly fell over her again. He didn't say a word but pushed her into the coal-cellar and shut the door firmly. "You'll be out of my way in there," he whispered, when he had banged the door. The cat settled down on the coal and began to wash herself. She quite liked the coal-cellar.

But still Mrs. Twiddle wouldn't forgive poor Twiddle. She ate her tea in silence. She wouldn't look at him. It was really dreadful.

Twiddle couldn't eat anything, he was so upset. What else could he do to show his little wife that he was very sorry? He sat and thought. Then he got up and took down his hat and coat. "I'm going to take the poor dog for a run," he said. "I'll fetch him from his kennel."

The rain was pelting against the windows, and Twiddle did hope that Mrs. Twiddle would say no, he wasn't to go out in such a downpour. But she didn't. She just sat and drank her tea and wouldn't even *look* at poor Twiddle! So out he went into the rain and darkness, and made his way to the kennel.

Rain or not, the dog was very glad to see him. He would hardly stand still for Twiddle to put on his lead. In the end Twiddle dropped it on the ground and couldn't find it again in the darkness. Oh, dear! He really didn't want to go back into the house to get a torch to look for the lead. So he took a bit of rope and tied that through the dog's collar instead.

He set off with the dog in the rain. He hadn't got an umbrella, so he soon got wet. He was hungry and thirsty because he hadn't had any tea. He was also very miserable. So was the dog, because he didn't think walks in the rain and darkness were much fun—and he didn't like a silent, unhappy master.

Twiddle soon came to the town. He came to a

brightly lit little place called "Tilly's Tea-Room." A nice smell of toast came out from the door. It made Mr. Twiddle feel very hungry indeed. He knew this tea-room. It was a place where farmers came after market to have tea and toast and new-baked ginger cake. Outside was a strong railing to which they could tie their horses, cows, a sheep or two, and dogs.

Twiddle decided to go in and have some tea and toast. He tied the dog firmly to the railings by his rope. "Shan't be long, old fellow," he said. "It's stopped raining now so you'll be all right."

Twiddle enjoyed his tea and toast and new ginger cake. Then he thought he had better be getting back because Mrs. Twiddle might think he was out too long. So he paid his bill and got up to go.

It was pitch dark outside now. Twiddle wished and wished he had brought a torch. He groped his way to the railings and fell over what seemed to be a pig, by its excited grunts. He felt about for his dog.

"Where are you?" he said, and the dog barked

gladly. Twiddle undid the rope from the railing and set off home.

"Come along," he said. "We'll get back. I shall be glad of my warm fire and you'll be glad of your cosy kennel."

He walked home quickly, glad that it had stopped raining. He took the dog to its kennel and shut it in, giving it a push because it didn't seem to want to go in. Then he went indoors, hoping that Mrs. Twiddle was in a better temper now.

But she wasn't. "Where's the cat?" she asked him. "I can hear her yowling, but I can't find her."

Twiddle remembered where she was—oh, dear, in the coal-cellar! He went to the door and listened. Yes—she was yowling loudly. Then he heard another noise, too—one that puzzled him.

"Hiss-ss-ss! Hiss-ss-ss-ss!"

"What in the world is *that* noise?" asked Mrs. Twiddle, surprised.

"Sounds like a large snake, or something."

"HISS-SS-SS-SS!"

"Whatever can it be?" said Mrs. Twiddle stepping back quickly. "Gracious—if there's an escaped snake in the garden I shall scream the place down."

Twiddle was just about to shut the door when they heard another noise—a loud cackling, angry and fierce. Mrs. Twiddle looked most alarmed.

"Why—is there a goose out in the garden with the snake?" she asked. "Oh, Twiddle, dear Twiddle, I do feel frightened. Please do go and get the dog—he'll soon scare away any creatures that shouldn't be about."

Twiddle was pleased to hear himself being called "dear" again, but he didn't much like going out into the darkness among snakes and geese that seemed suddenly to have arrived from nowhere. The cat yowled loudly again.

"Let the cat in, too, wherever she is," said Mrs. Twiddle. "Do go on, Twiddle. Aren't you brave enough?"

Twiddle didn't really think he was—but he didn't feel that he could possibly risk making Mrs. Twiddle cross again, so out he went in the darkness, very valiantly.

He went to the coal-cellar and let out the cat, which flew past him with a loud screech.

Then, hoping that he wouldn't tread on a hissing snake or bump into a fierce goose, he went to the dog's kennel. He thought that he would feel much better with the dog beside him. He opened the kennel door and called the dog.

"Come on, old fellow, come on!"

He felt a sharp pain in his hand and drew back, shocked. "You bit me!" he said. "You bad dog! You bit your own master! Come on out."

But the dog wouldn't come out. Instead that peculiar hissing noise came again. Twiddle scurried away in terror.

"The snake's in the kennel with the dog—and the dog bit me!" he shouted to his wife. Mrs. Twiddle was most astonished.

"The dog *bit* you!" she said. "Our own dear gentle dog! I don't believe it. I shall go out at once with the torch and bring him in myself, snakes or no snakes!"

And out she went, shining the torch bravely in front of her. Twiddle followed her. They came to the kennel and Mrs. Twiddle shone her torch in to see the dog. She gave such a loud cry of alarm and astonishment that Twiddle almost scuttled back to the house again.

"Twiddle! Look—what's this in our dog's kennel? Oh, TWIDDLE! IT'S A GOOSE!"

And sure enough an enormous goose poked out her head and cackled and hissed loudly at Mrs.

Twiddle. She pushed it back and shut the kennel door on it. She went back to the house with Twiddle, marvelling at the goose in the kennel.

"A goose! A *goose*! However did it get in the dog's kennel? And where is the dog? No wonder we thought there were snakes about when that goose hissed! Twiddle, did *you* put that goose into the kennel?"

Twiddle was just about to say no, of *course* not, how could he—when a dreadful thought came into his head.

Could he *possibly* have untied a goose from that railing, instead of his dog? It had been so dark that he might have got the ropes muddled and taken someone else's goose and left his poor old dog. Yes—he remembered now—the goose had felt very soft when he had pushed what he thought was his dog, into the kennel. It must have been a goose.

He had brought back somebody's goose! Oh, dear, oh, dear!

"Maybe I brought back a goose instead of the dog," he said. "I stopped and had tea at a tea-room and tied the dog up outside. Now don't you say a word, wife—I'll take back the goose and find our dog."

So out went poor Twiddle into the rain and darkness again, pulling the surprised and angry goose behind him. How he hoped his dog was still there!

And at home Mrs. Twiddle was staring angrily at the cat, who was lying on a clean cushion making it absolutely black with coal-dust from the coal-cellar! Her paws and fur were black with it.

"And where have *you* been, I should like to know?" she said. "Sitting in the cellar again, I suppose? How many times have I chased you out of there? You bad animal! Out you go and get yourself clean in the rain!"

And when Twiddle came home with the dog he was met by the cat, flying angrily out of the door with Mrs. Twiddle chasing it. Twiddle was pleased. He never had liked his wife's cat.

"Bring the poor dog in and dry him. And dry yourself too, Twiddle," said Mrs. Twiddle in a kind voice. "I'll make you some hot cocoa. That cat must have been in the coal-cellar again! Just *look* at my nice clean cushion!"

Twiddle looked, but he didn't say a word. He wasn't going to risk making Mrs. Twiddle cross all over again by explaining how the cat got into the coal-cellar. It was nice to see her smiling once more. He and the dog could snuggle up peacefully together by the fire.

They did—and will you believe it, Twiddle is fast asleep again! And so is the dog.

13

Mr. Twiddle and the Dogs

"It's a very funny thing, Twiddle," said Mrs. Twiddle, "but I always notice that if anyone ever brings a dog here, it never goes to *you*. It always makes a fuss of *me*."

Mr. Twiddle felt cross. "It's merely because *you* make a fuss of the dog," he said. "Anyway, my love, you always make such a dreadful fuss of our cat that it has quite turned me against making a fuss of any creature, dog, cat or horse."

"That's not the true reason," said Mrs. Twiddle, indignantly. "You know perfectly well that cats don't like you, and dogs don't either. I don't think that's very nice, Twiddle. I think there must be something wrong with you."

Mr. Twiddle put down his newspaper. "There's NOTHING wrong with me," he said. "I do like cats, but ours makes such a habit of tripping me up that I don't see why I should make a fuss of her. And I do like dogs, but, as I say, surely one person going crazy over any dog-visitor is enough. I've no doubt all the dogs would come to me if you didn't make such a fuss of them that they don't even know I'm here!"

"Very well," said Mrs. Twiddle. "Very well, Twiddle. The very next time any dog comes I will hardly take any notice of it at all—but you'll see, it will still come to me and not to you."

"You are quite wrong, my love," said Twiddle, and began to read his newspaper again.

"Now listen, Twiddle," said Mrs. Twiddle. "I'm certain I'm right and you're certain I'm wrong. Very well—if I prove right you must give me a new hat. And if you prove right I'll give you a new scarf."

Mr. Twiddle didn't like the sound of that at all. He had a kind of feeling that all dogs would go fawning round dear, kind, plump little Mrs. Twiddle. There was something about her that animals and children couldn't resist. He sighed.

"Why do you pester me so? Very well—I'll buy you a new hat if you're right. Now, do let me read my newspaper, and stop talking about dogs."

Mr. Twiddle didn't really think much more

about all this till he saw his wife looking at a hat catalogue—and to his horror he noticed that she had put a cross beside a very pretty hat. Goodness gracious, it was three pounds and five shillings! Mr. Twiddle began to feel alarmed.

"Suppose she makes me buy such a very expensive hat?" he thought. "I wouldn't be able to buy any tobacco for my pipe for

WRT—*

about three months. This will never do. I must think hard."

So he thought hard for a day or two, and then he suddenly stopped looking worried. He felt that he knew what to do. So he went to the butcher and bought a nice threepenny bone that just fitted neatly into his right-hand trouser-pocket without showing. He put it there, and patted it. Aha! Dogs would feel very friendly towards him now!

That very day his wife's sister came, bringing with her a little yappy poodle. "Oh, the darling!" said Mrs. Twiddle, and held out her hands to it.

It began to run to her—but half-way to Mrs. Twiddle it stopped and sniffed. What was that Perfectly Delicious Smell coming from over on the right, where that man was sitting with his newspaper? Sniff-sniff! Lovely smell!

The dog dodged away from Mrs. Twiddle and ran to Mr. Twiddle. Ah—the smell was here! It leapt straight up on to Twiddle's knee and began to lick him.

"Well, I never!" said Mrs. Twiddle, astonished. "Look at that!"

Twiddle smiled broadly. He put the dog down. "Go to Missus, then," he said. "Go to Missus and say how-de-do!"

But no—the dog only wanted to be near this exciting bone-smell.

Where was it? It leapt up again on to Mr. Twiddle and made a fuss of him.

"I'm afraid that's one up to you, Twiddle," said Mrs. Twiddle, surprised and not very pleased. "What a very peculiar thing!"

"Not at all. Probably likes my smell," said Twiddle truthfully, and pushed the dog away again.

The next day old Mrs. Dally came in, bringing with her a rather muddy spaniel. "Oh, the dear boy!" cooed Mrs. Twiddle. "The beautiful, long-eared boy!"

But the beautiful long-eared boy didn't give her even a glance. It gave one delightful sniff and flew to Mr. Twiddle. Forty pounds of very muddy, rather smelly dog leapt on to his plump knees, and licked him vigorously from hair to chin. Mr. Twiddle fended him off.

"Don't! Oooh, you're a very drippy dog. Take your tongue away from my nose. I've already washed my face once this morning. Go away, I tell you! You smell!"

"Funny that my darling doggy has taken such a

fancy to your husband when he doesn't like dogs, isn't it?" said Mrs. Dally, who wasn't pleased to hear her dog called smelly.

"It is queer," agreed Mrs. Twiddle, puzzled and rather upset. Could it be that Mr. Twiddle really did attract dogs after all? Look at that spaniel now—snuffing all over him, sniff-snuff-sniffle-snuffle! Why, anyone would think it was his own dog!

The spaniel could smell the bone in Mr. Twiddle's trouser-pocket and was thrilled. It scrabbled and scraped at him, licking him and flapping its long ears about till Twiddle could bear it no longer. He rose suddenly from his chair and the dog fell to the floor.

"If there's one thing worse than a man making a silly fuss of a dog, it's a dog making a silly fuss of a man!" he said. "Now, wife, perhaps you'll say I'm right and you're wrong—dogs do prefer me!"

"They certainly seem to," said Mrs. Twiddle. "Oh, dear—now I'll have to buy you the scarf and go without that dear little hat!"

Mr. Twiddle looked at her. Well, if she was going to buy him a scarf, he *would* buy her a hat—but not that very expensive one—oh, no!

"Listen, my love," he said. "You can buy me the scarf, as I am right and you are wrong; but I'll buy *you* a hat, though *not* more than thirty shillings will I spend! Just to show you that I'm a kind and generous husband!"

"Oh, you are, you are!" cried Mrs. Twiddle, and she ran to hug him. The spaniel leapt at them both, still trying to get to Mr. Twiddle's trouser-pocket. That bone! Oh, how good it smelt!

"Well, I *still* can't understand my doggy making a fuss of Mr. Twiddle," said Mrs. Dally, annoyed. "He's never done that before."

Now, the next day, Mr. and Mrs. Twiddle set off to buy the scarf and the hat. They bought the scarf, a nice dark-blue one with white spots. Mr. Twiddle fancied himself very much in it. Then they went off to the hat shop.

Now, on the way, who should they meet but little Mr. Trot with his great big Alsatian dog. Mrs. Twiddle always said she didn't know if Mr.

Trot was taking the dog for a walk, or if the dog
was taking Mr. Trot for one.

Mr. Twiddle suddenly remembered the bone in

his trouser-pocket. He had forgotten to take it out! He began to cross the road in a hurry, before the Alsatian could smell it. But Mrs. Twiddle pulled him back.

"We must just have a word with Mr. Trot, dear," she said. "And we *must* pat his lovely Alsatian."

Mr. Twiddle didn't want to do anything of the sort, but it was too late to retreat now. The great dog had already caught a whiff of the rather smelly bone. It bounded at Mr. Twiddle with a bark of welcome and almost knocked him over. Little Mr. Trot was pulled violently along on the lead.

"Get down, you brute! Hey, get down! Stop it! Don't poke me in the face with your clumsy paws!" yelled Mr. Twiddle, fending the big dog away. But the Alsatian was certain that Mr. Twiddle was a long-lost friend, a friend with a delicious bony smell, someone who would very soon produce the bone, if only the Alsatian could make a big enough fuss of him.

Mr. Trot tugged at the lead. The dog took no notice. He leapt at Mr. Twiddle again, his tongue

out, and Mr. Twiddle went down like a skittle. Bang! He was full-length on the pavement, squirming away from the excited dog.

Mrs. Twiddle was absolutely astounded to see a dog making such a fuss of Twiddle—even knocking him over in his affection! Good gracious! But she didn't like to see Twiddle on the ground, so she poked the dog with her umbrella.

"Stop it, stop it! Let him get up!"

The Alsatian was worrying at Twiddle's right-hand trouser-pocket. He tore it. He snapped at the bone there and pulled it out, together with Twiddle's handkerchief, a tobacco pouch and a ten-shilling note. Woof! What a bone!

After that Mr. Trot found it easy to manage his enormous dog. The Alsatian was quite willing to trot home quietly, with his smelly bone, and off he went, dragging his little master behind him.

Mrs. Twiddle helped Twiddle up. She looked at him very crossly indeed. "*I* saw what you had in your pocket," she said. "A bone! You are a fraud, Twiddle. A great big shocking fraud! That's why the dogs made such a fuss of you—just because you put a bone in your pocket. I'm ashamed of you! You've got a new scarf out of me unfairly. You—you—you . . . oh, dear, I'm going to cry!"

But Twiddle couldn't bear that. He put his arm round plump little Mrs. Twiddle and gave her a squeeze.

"What are you crying for?" he said. "It was just a silly joke. Come on—we're going to buy that three-pound-five-shilling hat. Cheer up!"

So Mrs. Twiddle cheered up at once, and smiled happily. "You're a very silly man," she said. "Very silly indeed. But sometimes I think you're quite nice. Oh, Twiddle, *don't* go putting bones in your pocket again—you've no idea how they will make your clothes smell!"

"You needn't worry. I shall never do that again," said Twiddle, trotting along. "You can have all the fussy dogs there are. I don't want ANY!"

14

Mr. Twiddle gets a Surprise

"I'M just going out, my love!" Mr. Twiddle called to Mrs. Twiddle.

"Twiddle! Now don't you forget the fish for the cat!" called Mrs. Twiddle, running to the front door. "And pay the bill at the newspaper shop. And goodness, don't you want a basket for the fish? You know how you make your coat smell if you come home clutching the packet of fish to your chest!"

"Dear me, yes—I must have a basket," said Twiddle. His wife ran to get it. When she came back she had his mackintosh with her, too. "It's going to rain," she said. "You had better take this, too, Twiddle."

Twiddle set off, his mackintosh over one arm, and the basket swinging in his hand. He met Mr. Grin and had a nice little talk with him. He met Miss Hurry, but she was gone before he could say more than "Good morning."

As he passed the cake-shop a very nice smell of

hot scones came out. Twiddle stopped and sniffed. "I think I'll pop in and have a cup of hot coffee and a scone or two," he thought. "I really didn't have much breakfast."

So in he went and chose a table. Soon he was sipping a cup of coffee and eating a whole plate of warm, buttered scones. Very nice, indeed!

He heard a noise outside and looked out of the window. "There now!" he said. "Mrs. Twiddle was right—it's raining! What a good thing I've got my mac. It's simply pouring down!"

He paid his bill, picked up his basket, and went to get his mac from the peg near-by. "Now, let me see—what did I have to get?" he wondered. "What *was* it now? Fish for breakfast? Fetch the papers? Call at the cleaners? What shopping did I have to do?"

He struggled into his mac and went out into the rain. Bother! What was it his wife had told him to get? The rain splashed into his face, and he groped in his pocket for a handkerchief.

He brought out a nice clean one, still folded tidily. Nice Mrs. Twiddle! She had even put a clean hanky in his pocket for him! He felt something else there as well, and pulled it out.

Oh, *good*! A shopping list! Now he didn't need to try and remember what he had to get. Dear Mrs. Twiddle had written it all down and he couldn't possibly make a mistake! He heaved a sigh of relief.

He put his hand in the other pocket and found his pipe there—and a small tin of his tobacco. How

very, very kind of Mrs. Twiddle. Mr. Twiddle felt
very loving towards her and made up his mind to
buy her some roses. She was very fond of roses.

He lighted his pipe and looked at the list of
shopping. It was rather a long one—no wonder
Mrs. Twiddle had written it all out, instead of
leaving it to him to remember! Ha—herrings for
breakfast—he *thought* there was something about
fish! Tooth-paste—cotton-wool—he must go to
the chemist for those. And what was this?

"Nice big bone," read Twiddle. "That's a bit
funny. Oh, I expect she wants it for soup. Sausages
—well, I can get those at the butcher's too. And,
dear me—a *coal-hammer!* Well, well—does Mrs.
Twiddle expect me to break up those big lumps of
coal? She hasn't said a *word* to me about it!"

"Chocolate cake" came next on the list. Mr.
Twiddle beamed. He liked chocolate cake, and
Mrs. Twiddle hardly ever bought one because, she
said, they were too dear. And look at this—six
crumpets! If there was one thing Mr. Twiddle
liked more than another it was toasted crumpets
for tea!

"No wonder Mrs. Twiddle told me to take a basket," he thought. "Well, well—what a lot of shopping—but very *nice* shopping, I must say. Chocolate cake—crumpets—sausages. Well, I hope *those* are for supper."

Twiddle went off happily, smoking his pipe. He must certainly remember to buy some roses for Mrs. Twiddle now. After all, she was going to give him such nice meals, she deserved some roses!

He went to the fish-monger's and bought some herrings. Ha, he would enjoy those! He went to the chemist and bought his favourite tooth-paste and nice big packet of cotton-wool.

When he came out of the chemist's shop he found it had stopped raining, so he took off his mac and folded it neatly over his arm.

"Now to the butcher for a big bone," said Twiddle, quite enjoying himself. "And the saus-ages, too. Look at them, all looped round the front of his shop."

He came out of the butcher's shop with two big bones and a pound of pork sausages. Then he went off to the ironmonger's and bought a really

fine coal-hammer. "This will break up those big lumps of coal quite easily!" he thought, and swung it up and down in the air.

"Now then, now then!" said a voice just behind him. "You nearly hit me on the nose!"

It was Mr. Surly, so Twiddle said he was very, very sorry, he was just trying out his coal-hammer to see how it would break up big lumps of coal.

"You're lucky to *have* coal," said Mr. Surly. "We've only got wood. And fancy having lumps big enough to break up! Where did you get them from?"

Mr. Twiddle had no idea, and as he didn't at all like Mr. Surly, he popped into the shop that sold crumpets and got rid of Mr. Surly that way.

He bought the biggest chocolate cake he could see and six lovely crumpets with holes in them that made them look just like flat sponges.

By this time his basket was very, very full, and he staggered homewards with it.

Last of all he bought three beautiful red roses. "Red roses mean 'I love you,'" said Twiddle to himself, pleased. "Aha! Mrs. Twiddle will like those!"

He got home and went indoors. Mrs. Twiddle was in the kitchen. Twiddle tip-toed into the sitting-room, got a vase, filled it with water and put the three red roses into it. He left them in the middle of the table for Mrs. Twiddle to see. He called her.

"I'm in the kitchen!" she cried. "Just baking a cake. Come in here to me, Twiddle."

Twiddle went in with his basket. "I've done all the shopping," he said. "Quite a lot, too, there was."

"Oh, no, Twiddle dear—there wasn't very much," said Mrs. Twiddle, busy at the oven.

"Meow," said the cat, smelling the fish and coming over to rub herself against Mr. Twiddle's legs.

"Don't," said Twiddle. "You make the ankles of my trousers all hairy. How many times have I told you not to do that, Cat?"

"I expect she smells the fish you've brought her," said Mrs. Twiddle, looking into her oven.

"Fish for the cat? You said herrings for breakfast!" said Twiddle, in alarm.

"I didn't!" said Mrs. Twiddle. "We've got kippers for breakfast. You bought them yourself yesterday. *Don't* say you've got herrings as well. Really, Twiddle! Did you pay the bill at the newspaper shop? I gave you the money for it."

"Er—no. Dear me, that wasn't on the list," said

Twiddle, feeling muddled. "Yes—I do remember your asking me now. But . . ."

"Oh, Twiddle! That's the second time you've forgotten to pay that bill," said Mrs. Twiddle, banging the oven door.

"Well, I remembered EVERYTHING ELSE," said Twiddle. "Here are the bones for soup—and the sausages. . . ."

"Bones for soup? Are you mad, Twiddle?" said his little wife. "I never said a word about bones for soup."

"Oh well—perhaps you wanted bones for that dog next door you're so fond of," said Twiddle huffily. "How was I to know? And you *did* say sausages—it was down on . . ."

Mrs. Twiddle was now taking the things out of his basket in amazement. "Bones—and pork sausages—and herrings. No wonder the cat was interested in your basket and came to make a fuss of you!"

She lifted out the chocolate cake and the crumpets. "Goodness me! What in the world did you go and get these for? I *told* you I was baking cakes to-day! Twiddle, I really begin to think you've gone mad!"

She took out the tooth-paste and the cotton-wool. "And look at these! You had a new tube of tooth-paste yesterday—and, why all this cotton-wool? Are you going to stuff a cushion or something? And TWIDDLE! Is that a coal-hammer? Oh, Twiddle, you'll be the death of me! You know we haven't any coal—only a bit of coke and some wood!"

"Well," began Twiddle, most annoyed, "all these things were down on your . . ."

"Twiddle! You must have spent all the money I gave you for the newspaper bill on these things!" said Mrs. Twiddle. "It was my *housekeeping* money!

It was very wrong of you to do that. You can pay
for them all out of your own money!"

Twiddle was most alarmed. "But I can't. I only
have enough to . . ."

Mrs. Twiddle burst into tears. "Why did you
get all those things? Now I shall never, *never* be
able to trust you to go shopping again."

There came a knock at the front door just then.
Twiddle went to see who it was, feeling very
gloomy indeed. A tall man stood there, dressed in
a mackintosh. He beamed at Twiddle.

"I say," he said, "I'm very, very sorry—but I've
done something *so* silly."

Twiddle was very, very glad to hear that someone else could do silly things. He asked the man in
at once. "It's like this," said the man, standing in
the hall, "I went to have a cup of coffee at the tea-
shop—and by mistake I took your mac when I
went out. So I've brought it back. It had your
name in it. Did you by any chance take mine?
They are very alike!"

Mrs. Twiddle came out to hear what all the
talking was about. She looked at the mac Twiddle

had hung in the hall. "Yes—he took yours!" she said. "They *are* alike! Dear, dear—you men!"

"Good gracious!" said Twiddle, light dawning on him all at once. "I smoked your pipe, then—and used your hanky—and oh, my word, I bought all the things on your shopping list!"

"No! Did you really?" said the tall man. "You know, I tried to remember everything that was down, but I couldn't. I bought the chocolate cake and the crumpets—and I bought the bones for soup, and the sausages and the herrings. Was there anything else on the list?"

"Yes—tooth-paste—cotton-wool—and a coal-hammer," said Twiddle dolefully.

"My word!" said the man. "I forgot all those. I *shall* get into trouble when I get back home. But do you *want* tooth-paste and cotton-wool and a coal-hammer?"

"Of course not!" said Mrs. Twiddle, answering for Twiddle. "You can have them if you'd like to pay us for them."

"Oh, I will, with pleasure," said the man. "It will save me going back to the shops. Dear,

dear—I must have the worst memory in the
world."

"Yes—even worse than mine," agreed Twiddle
happily. "Here's the hammer—tooth-paste—and
cotton-wool."

"I'm sorry you bought the other things," said
the man, paying out the money. "But I've bought
them, too, and I really couldn't face my wife with
two chocolate cakes, *two* lots of sausages, *two* . . ."

"No, no, of course not," said Twiddle, who
was not at all anxious to hand over the cake, the
crumpets and the rest.

The man took off Twiddle's mac, and Twiddle
gave him the right one. They said good-bye, and
out he went, his basket full.

Mrs. Twiddle still looked very cross. Twiddle
knew she had a lot more to say.

"Come into the sitting-room, Twiddle," said
Mrs. Twiddle, in a stern voice. "I have something
to say to you." He followed her in, feeling very
gloomy. She suddenly saw the three red roses in
the vase.

"Wherever did those lovely flowers come

from?" said Mrs. Twiddle, and sniffed them in
delight.

"I bought them for you," said Twiddle, in a
small voice.

"Red roses mean 'I love you,'" said Mrs.
Twiddle, her eyes shining.

"That's why I bought them," said Twiddle.
"I may be a very silly husband, but I do think

you are a nice little wife. So I bought you those roses."

"Twiddle, you're a darling!" said Mrs. Twiddle, and she gave him a very sudden hug. "Now, when would you like the sausages? For supper? And I'll make some nice soup with those bones. And herrings will do fine for breakfast, because the kippers will keep. And we'll have a little tea-party with those lovely crumpets and chocolate cake!"

Well, well, well! Twiddle simply couldn't understand the sudden change. But I can, can't you? After all, if somebody loves you very much, you can put up with quite a lot of silliness! Dear old Twiddle, I can't help liking him.